DR KILDARE TAKES CHARGE

DR KILDARE TAKES CHARGE

Max Brand™

Chivers Press • G.K. Hall & Co.
Bath, Avon, England • Thorndike, Maine USA

This Large Print edition is published by Chivers Press, England, and by G.K. Hall & Co., USA.

Published in 1997 in the U.K. by arrangement with the author's estate and Golden West Literary Agency.

Published in 1997 in the U.S. by arrangement with Golden West Literary Agency.

U.K. Hardcover ISBN 0–7451–6952–X (Chivers Large Print)
U.K. Softcover   ISBN 0–7451–6964–3 (Camden Large Print)
U.S. Softcover   ISBN 0–7833–1848–5 (Nightingale Collection Edition)

The text of this Large Print edition is unabridged.
Other aspects of the book may vary from the original edition.

Set in 16 pt. New Times Roman.

Printed in Great Britain on acid-free paper.

British Library Cataloguing in Publication Data available

Library of Congress Cataloging-in-Publication Data

Brand, Max, 1892–1944.
  Dr. Kildare takes charge / Max Brand.
    p.   cm.
  ISBN 0–7838–1847–5 (lg. print : sc)
  1. Kildare, Doctor (Fictitious character)—Fiction.   2. Physicians—United States—Fiction.   3. Large type books.   I. Title.
[PS3511.A87D68   1997]
813'.52—dc20

96–20901

CONTENTS

CONTENTS

CHAPTER ONE

YOU CAN BE DOCTORS

When the head of the hospital, that hard-faced Roman, Doctor Carew, joined himself to their famous diagnostician, Leonard Gillespie, the rest of the staff prepared itself for something important.

As the cortege moved down the hall, the way was led by the wheel-chair of that white-haired old lion, Gillespie, who always looked as if he had just finished one battle and was hurrying to get into another fight.

Carew walked at one side of him and on the other was Doctor Stephen Kildare, whose age and country practice seemed to appear in the cut of his threadbare clothes.

Behind the chair was young Doctor Kildare, carrying a sheaf of charts. Nurse Mary Lamont now hurried ahead to open the door to an infants' ward.

'Wait a minute,' said Gillespie. 'Kildare!'

'Yes, sir,' said young Kildare.

'Back up,' said Gillespie. 'I don't mean you, babyface. I mean somebody of importance. Doctor Kildare,' he went on to the father, 'before we go in there to look your experiment in the face, I'm going to tell you that if it runs on as well as it's started, I intend to publish

1

your results.'

'Publish? Publish?' murmured old Kildare. 'No, Gillespie. It's kind of you but I wouldn't know what to do with a public appearance. I mean to say—'

'You and your modesty are out of this,' said Gillespie. 'In a small way it would make you famous, perhaps; but the main lesson is that country practitioners could benefit the whole world, as well as their patients, now and then, if they'd do what you've done: take notes on their work and their results.

'The work of all our doctors every day, with ten minutes to note it down, would be like the rain in the mountains that works its way to the sea, sooner or later—rivers of sound information, Kildare, to sweep filthy disease away and give us a clean world.

'But confound them they won't take time to make notes... Give me one of your books, Kildare!'

The old country doctor pulled out a small notebook and handed it over. Gillespie thumbed through a few of the crowded pages.

'Heaven help the man who had to read it,' he said, 'but just the same this is the sword that will win our battle for us. What started the good habit for you?'

'A bad, tricky memory,' confessed the old man, and laughed a little, ashamed of himself, as they went on into the ward so filled with sun and whiteness, that it glowed like a crystal.

'Here we are with the seedlings,' said Gillespie, looking over the row of bassinets. 'How quickly they grow up into trees, Kildare, and blights hit them in the leaf and the branch, until at last they decay at the root and go back to the earth that made 'em.'

'After bearing a little fruit, now and then?' suggested old Kildare.

'That's where Jimmy gets it, eh?' demanded Gillespie. 'That crackpot optimism of his that's always seeing saints and heroes wrapped up in human hides... What's the matter with you now, young Doctor Kildare? What are you scowling about? Have I stepped on one of your sore toes? Can't you take it?'

'It's *that* that bothers me,' said Kildare, pointing, and with his head canted a little to the side.

'What's he talking about?' asked Gillespie.

'It's the baby crying in the isolation ward next door,' said Nurse Lamont.

It was rather a rhythm to be felt than a sound to be heard.

'I get it now,' said Gillespie. 'First time you've ever heard a baby crying, young Kildare?'

'I don't like it,' said Kildare.

'Well, if he doesn't like it, why doesn't somebody do something about it?' demanded Gillespie. 'What's the case, Jimmy?'

'Undernourishment, to begin with,' said Kildare. 'But there's an acutely infected throat,

3

also, and the lab report is negative for a streptococcic infection.'

'Look at that girl, doctor,' said Gillespie to old Kildare, as he pointed out Mary Lamont. 'Every time your son speaks, she looks as if a bird were singing. Might be a swan-song, one of these days. Wipe off that silly look, Lamont, and go check the sore throat in that ward.'

As she hurried off, he added: 'Getting so, around this hospital, that we don't even dare let the babies cry. Your boy mightn't like it.'

Carew said: 'We'll take one of the outstanding cases. Kildare, suggest one.'

Young Kildare said to the ward nurse: 'Let's have a look at Pete Douglas.'

'Yes, doctor,' she said, turning.

'Do you know *all* the names of the babies in this ward?' Carew asked the interne.

'I believe so, sir,' said Kildare.

The eye of the father brightened, but old Gillespie was snarling: 'Yes, he spreads himself all over the hospital. Spreads himself thin. Has to know everything. Nose into everything. Patients can't have any privacy around this man's hospital. I wish you'd find me a new assistant, Walter.'

'If I find one, you'll get rid of him in a day,' said Carew, faintly smiling. He added to old Kildare, 'How did you run into this cereal you've been using for baby formulae?'

'I ran into it in my kitchen,' said the country doctor, with his mind and his eye still half on

4

his son. 'My wife cooked it; her mother had cooked it before her. Jimmy, here, was a scrawny baby; so I tried that cereal and it worked. I've kept on using it. It's not infallible but sometimes it turns the trick; and I've been keeping up with the vitamins of late years. They seemed to help.'

'Listen to these brats crowing,' said Gillespie. 'Not like a ward of sick children at all. More like bull-frogs singing on a summer evening. What kind of bull-frogs d'you have out there in Dartford, doctor?'

'All matched voices,' said old Kildare. 'You should hear 'em! Nothing but close harmony.'

'I'd *like* to hear 'em,' said Gillespie, 'if you'll ever give me a chance and ask me out there... Give me that baby, nurse!'

The nurse had returned with a small infant in her arms; she laid it in the lap of the diagnostician. It was a scrawny little specimen with a mist of red hair. It clenched its fists, now, and writhed its mouth wide open, ready to yell.

'Shut your mouth and lie still, Pete,' said Gillespie.

'Look!' murmured the nurse, amazed, for Pete Douglas changed his mind about wailing and began to gape, open-mouthed, at the ugly old face of Gillespie.

'What's there to look at?' demanded Gillespie. 'It'd be a pretty strange thing if I couldn't keep a Scotch baby from crying, wouldn't it? Tell me about this weighty

Douglas, Jimmy.'

'He's six months old,' said young Kildare. 'He came in here ten days ago badly dehydrated and we couldn't make him hold liquids. I tried father's formula. He's put on three pounds already.'

'Good!' said Carew.

'Good? Not at all!' said Gillespie. 'It's only barely medium, considering that he's a Scotch baby... Kildare,' he added, turning to the country doctor, 'I *am* going to publish you and your grandma's cereal, whether you like it or not.'

'Why—' began old Kildare, embarrassed and pleased.

'No, sir,' cut in the son. 'Not yet. We've still got to learn a lot about it.'

'You see?' said Gillespie, pointing. 'He thinks that there's only one doctor in his family. Well, he's right, and the one doctor isn't he. What's the matter? Why can't we publish results like this, young man?'

'We've had some failures,' said Jimmy. 'And Father hasn't cleaned up the record of the last three years. It's still in his notebooks.'

'Will you give us that stuff, then?' asked Gillespie.

'I'll have it all in the mail inside of a week,' he answered.

Mary Lamont came rather breathlessly back into the ward. There followed her a tall, gloomy young man who wore a striped apron.

6

'What's this? Some kitchen help?' asked Gillespie.

'It's a new report on that throat case in the isolation ward,' said the nurse.

'Who are you?' demanded Gillespie.

'Davison, sir,' said the tall young man. 'I'm the media man, in the laboratory, sir.'

'I thought you looked something like a cook,' said Gillespie. 'Did Doctor Kearns give you the report for us? Let me have some details.'

'The first swab didn't give altogether satisfactory results. It was a throat swab, sir. There were some organisms that seemed to resemble diphtheria bacilli.'

'Is that what Kearns said?'

'Dr Kearns was busy at the moment.'

'So you took over and went ahead?'

'Yes, sir. I looked up the patient and got a nose swab. The results are perfectly clear. I spread the swab on Loffler's media and incubated it. The diphtheria bacillus was there.'

'Diphtheria. I remember when that was a word to curdle the spinal marrow of a doctor,' said Gillespie. 'But I want to know something else, Davison.'

'Yes, sir.'

'Why the devil did Doctor Kearns turn over delicate and important work like this to you?'

'I specialised somewhat in this work, sir.'

'Yes, yes. As a laboratory worker, very

7

good, very good. Commendable industry and all that. But why in thunder does Kearns let this work be done by anyone other than a full-fledged doctor?'

'I *am* a doctor, sir,' said Davison.

'A doctor? In a fifteen dollar a week laboratory job?' growled Gillespie.

'No, it's eighteen dollars, sir.'

Gillespie closed his eyes.

'What is your school, doctor?' he asked.

'Columbia, sir.'

'Trouble with your studies?'

'Not particularly.'

'Where did you stand in your class?'

'Number three, sir.'

'Afterwards you hung out your shingle and no patients came?'

'That was it, sir.'

'I'm going to remember you, Davison,' said Gillespie. 'Though I don't know what good my thinking will do. How many millions of Americans practically do without medical service, and how many ten thousands of young doctors fold up because they can't get started?'

'Look, Carew! Here's the desert; and here's water. Bring the two together and you have life. But what can be done when—'

His voice stopped short; his hand paused in the middle of a gesture; for Pete Douglas had caught at Gillespie's forefinger and was holding it now in a strong and delighted grip.

There was a good deal of laughter over this.

8

Under cover of it Kildare stepped up to Davison, who had drawn gradually back from the group as if he could not tell whether it were time to linger or leave.

Kildare said: 'What's the matter, Jack? You look white. You look sick. Anything wrong with Joan?'

'She's pretty well,' murmured Davison. 'It was only the way Gillespie glowered at me. I thought for a minute that my job was going out the window.'

'It won't go out of the window,' said Kildare, staring at him and seeing things that did not meet the eye. 'Another three weeks before the baby arrives?'

The gloomy face of Davison lighted. 'That's right,' he said. 'You're the one that remembers things, Jimmy!'

Then Gillespie was making an uproar about something, with another infant in his arms that laughed through the storm. Kildare went back to him slowly.

This fellow Davison was getting something almost like hope and happiness out of eighteen dollars a week; twenty odd years of education repaid with eighteen dollars a week—two people crowded into a single room and a third life now to be crammed into the same quarters—and all of this happening to a man of real talent, a man of genius, perhaps.

It entered Kildare like a shadow; it made his heart as cold as a stone. The chill of it never

9

would leave him so long as he had to remember the frightened face of Davison, the wan smiling of Joan.

There was a call for Dr Carew. He was wanted at once in his office.

'You people have the luck,' he said. 'You can be doctors. I'm only an office boy... Kildare, I want to talk some more about this. Come along with me and bring those charts...'

'Get the rest of the reports and bring them on to Carew's office,' said Kildare to Mary Lamont. 'He's going to be full of questions.'

CHAPTER TWO

ORANGE JUICE FOR TWO

Carew, hurrying with his quick, short steps, was first through the ante-room of his office, so bent on getting to his telephone that he had no eye for the people who were waiting.

But Kildare took note of a boy of eighteen or nineteen and a girl not much younger who rose up quickly from their chairs and with a frightened expectancy watched Carew cross the room.

Carew's secretary said: 'Your son is here, doctor.'

'Let him wait,' snapped Carew, throwing

open the door of his inner office.

The girl and boy sat down again, slowly, glancing at one another with pain and with relief mingled, as if some necessary operation had been postponed. Their hands touched and that covert gesture conveyed a long message to Kildare.

He carried her picture with him into the office where Carew already was snatching up a telephone. She was rather a pretty girl with high-arched, old-fashioned eyebrows, and there was nothing of 1941 about her. She seemed to have been created in an earlier age of stillness and of more quiet thought.

Sometimes a human life is written with an indelible ink that strikes almost through the page; but others, however charming, are in fragile characters, easily erased. She was like that, Kildare thought: easily erased, too dimly printed in the world's fabric.

In the meantime he laid out the charts on the desk.

The secretary appeared at the door as Carew rang off from a telephone conversation.

'Your son wishes to know whether he should wait or come back another day?' she asked.

'Tell him another day,' answered Carew. 'No, let him come in now ... Families have no sense, Kildare. They think a father is an institution, not a human being ... Now let's have a look at the chart of this baby, this what's-his-name.'

11

'Pete Douglas? The chart is here.'

The door opened.

'Come in, Willie,' said Carew... 'Why should you bother trying to remember the names of the infants, Kildare?'

'I don't bother. But somehow names mean more to me than numbers. Besides, this Pete is a pretty tough fellow.'

'Was he very ill, Kildare?'

'*Very* ill, sir.'

'What formula was he on before you shifted him to your father's? ... Willie, what do you want?'

'I'm afraid that I'll have to talk to you alone,' said William Carew.

'Talk to me alone? Nonsense!' said Carew. 'This is only a doctor. This is our Dr Kildare. My son William, Kildare.'

Kildare went over a few steps and shook hands, smiling, but he could not melt the stiffness out of the strict attention at which William stood. He seemed very much afraid of his father but still more afraid of that which had driven him to the office.

There was nothing unusual about this lad except the sense that he was under the whip and bound somewhere. This case had to do with the mind alone, but it seemed to Kildare to need a quick diagnosis.

'You can talk right out, Willie,' the father was saying impatiently. 'You've heard of Kildare, haven't you?'

12

'I'm sorry,' answered William.

'Always wrong and always sorry,' commented Dr Carew. 'What? Never heard of Kildare, the people's friend? ... What did you say the first formula was, Kildare?'

'This one, sir,' explained Kildare, pointing it out on the chart. 'There's a protein content of fifteen per cent, carbohydrate seventy-one, fat, three, and minerals over three per cent.'

'Seems sound to me. But you changed it? ... Go on, go on, Willie! Let's have what's in your mind.'

There was no answer from William.

Kildare said: 'I've left half the report behind me. Sorry, sir. I'll come right back with it.'

He gathered the charts into a quick stack.

'Wait a minute—don't go, Kildare!' protested Carew.

'I'll be right back, sir, with the rest of it,' said Kildare, hurrying toward the door.

He threw a quick glance at William as he went and the eye of the boy brightened with understanding. Then Kildare was in the ante-room.

Mary Lamont, with a sheaf of reports, was already there, talking, or trying to talk, to the girl who waited for William Carew. It was like Mary to have found the right person. It made him feel, not for the first time, that some sort of telepathic communication existed between them.

As he came up, a side glance from Mary

13

indicated the girl to him as a person of importance.

'This is Dr Kildare, Marguerite Paston,' said Mary Lamont.

'How do you do, doctor?' said the soft voice of Marguerite Paston; but her whole mind was fixed on the closed door of Carew's office. Whatever happened to young Carew inside that door was obviously happening to her, also.

Mary Lamont gave over the reports; at the same time her significant eyes were begging Kildare to pay more attention to the girl beside her. She was saying: 'Paston is a *very* old English name, isn't it? Weren't they a great family back in the Middle Ages?'

The girl at last drew her attention away from the office door to answer: '*My* family is not great. We're simply West Siders. My uncle was Sammy Paston, the prizefighter.'

Mary Lamont caught her breath.

'Well, that's all right, isn't it?' asked Kildare.

'I think it may be,' said Marguerite Paston, with the same amazing frankness and quiet, 'but I was simply pointing out that I'm not of a great family.'

'You're not a West Sider,' said Kildare. 'They're all right, but you're not one of them.'

'I was born three blocks from the hospital,' she answered.

'But you've been away most of your life,' he insisted, though Mary Lamont was shaking

14

her head to indicate that this was the wrong track and that time was being wasted.

'I've been in a convent for a long time; that's why there's a difference in the way I talk,' she admitted. She seemed to care about nothing but truth and wanted to have it as naked as a new-born baby.

Mary Lamont, in the near background, made a gesture indicative of delight and bewilderment, inviting Kildare to see that this was a different sort of creature.

'I knew Sammy; I knew your uncle just before the end,' he said.

'Are you the one who took care of him?' she asked.

'I was one of them,' he said.

She stood up. She was rather small but there was something about her that made her quite tall enough.

'You're the one they all talk about; you're—the doc?' she said. 'I know you are. It's a sad sort of happiness, remembering all they've told me.'

She smiled at Kildare, faintly, and the smile took a long time to go out. Mary Lamont, very bright of face, continued to adore this grown-up child.

Then the door of Carew's office opened and young William stood on the threshold. Marguerite Paston forgot Kildare and all else as she listened, for the angry voice of Doctor Carew rang from his office, saying: 'And don't come back again until you've got this silly nonsense out of your head.'

William Carew waited, with the door still open, until his father had finished speaking his mind, though the boy must have known that everyone in the ante-room could hear what was said. After that he closed the door, turned slowly from it, and came on toward Marguerite.

He had the same look of tension that Kildare had noticed before, the same look of being under the whip and bound for a destination too far away to reach; but as he drew nearer to the girl he changed. He was even smiling as he picked up her coat and began to help her into it.

Mary Lamont, close to Kildare, was murmuring: 'She's lovely, Jimmy. Isn't she lovely? Did you ever see anyone half so lovely? They adore each other, don't they?'

'They do,' said Kildare through his teeth.

'What's the matter, Jimmy?'

'I don't know. There's something like murder in the air...'

Marguerite Paston was coming back to say goodbye to them, smiling.

'I want to talk to you,' said Kildare.

'Thank you, doctor,' replied young Carew, 'but there's a very important engagement ahead of us.'

'I'm *so* sorry,' agreed the girl.

'I know what your engagement is,' said Kildare.

'But you can't—' began William Carew.

'Hush!' said Marguerite to him, softly, as she watched Kildare.

'So you'll talk to me now, won't you?' asked Kildare.

'Yes, doctor,' said Marguerite.

He went out with them, past the startled questioning eyes of Mary Lamont.

'There's a back room in a saloon across the street,' said Kildare. 'Do you mind going to a place like that? We can be alone there.'

'I don't mind,' said the girl.

Young Carew continued to stare, bewildered. Then a loud speaker down the corridor announced: 'Doctor Kildare wanted in Doctor Gillespie's office. Urgent.'

'That's the great Gillespie and of course you'll have to go,' said Carew. He seemed relieved. 'We'll see you another time, doctor.'

The loud speaker repeated: 'Doctor Kildare wanted in Doctor Gillespie's office. Urgent!'

'This is more urgent than anything Gillespie has to do,' said Kildare, and his words straightened young Carew again. Only the girl seemed impervious to shock.

From the warmth of the hospital they passed out into New York's winter, grey as twilight, with a dust of freezing rain that drew the sky down to the city pavements.

A big truck loaded with fir trees went past them as they waited for a green light at the corner. It trailed a clean fragrance behind it.

17

'There goes Christmas,' said Kildare, surprised. He looked away into his thoughts. Every month since he came to the hospital had been longer than a long year.

The girl said: 'There aren't any seasons in a hospital year, I suppose.'

'That's good,' agreed Kildare. 'That's what I was thinking, without words.'

The boy watched the two of them, rather gravely amused to see someone else tasting the quality of Marguerite. So a collector shares his best vintage with a jealous delight.

As they went across the greasy street, Kildare was thinking that she had lived double her years in that quiet mind of hers. She was unlike Mary Lamont; for the Scotch girl was full of vigorous living, colour, and glow, like a brilliant oil painting; but the Paston girl was like a book of drawings, a little dim with time, in which the master has revealed himself.

If he loved Mary Lamont, everyone could understand his love and envy him. Her eye had the flash and her voice the sound to which men respond instantly. She was no abounding hoyden, at that, but she almost seemed one, compared with this quieter music.

'When you were born, your mother wasn't very young,' he said to her. The words slowed her nearly to a stop and she looked at him, he felt, for the first time.

'That's true,' she said. 'I was born old.'

She kept on looking at Kildare and at her

new conception of him. In any other person it would have been staring; but in her it meant simply that her mind was turned fully toward him.

As they reached the family entrance of Mike's saloon he said: 'This isn't the place for you; but it's the nearest.'

'Oh, but places don't matter, do they?' she asked.

He kept thinking of this as he opened the door and let them go in before him. The tawdriness of the back room of Ryan's place was freshly revealed to him. It was scrubbed up every day but soap and elbow-grease cannot always remove the uncleanness of time. It was like a woman's old hat, a dead fashion since the days when people liked varnish and gilt.

An uproar of two men in loud argument came from the bar even though the door between was closed. Kildare looked guiltily at the girl.

'It doesn't matter at all,' she said.

He pulled open the door. Mike himself was at it with Toppy Graham on the subject of the immortal long count over Tunney in the Chicago fight.

'Save it, Mike, will you?' asked Kildare. 'Maybe you're both right.'

'Sure, doc, sure!' said Mike Ryan. 'But there's no more sense in Toppy than there is in an old bell. It can't make only but one noise. Will you have something, doc?'

19

'Will you drink something?' Kildare asked them, turning.

They would have nothing. Mike came bustling from behind the bar to make sure. Said Toppy Graham: 'How's McAllister doin', doc?'

'Temperature's gone; he'll be all right,' said Kildare.

'We've been missing the old fool,' remarked Toppy. 'Will you have a look one day at my kid that's off his feed, doc? He was named after you.'

'He was named four years before you ever seen the doc, you lyin' liar, you,' said Mike.

'I would of changed the name if it hadn't been right, though,' said Toppy, calmly.

'Bring him around,' said Kildare. 'A beer for me, Mike, if you please.'

Mike had bundled himself through the doorway. He blinked and held up his hands when he saw the two who stood close together, utterly out of place.

'Ah, but look what we have here!'

'They don't want anything, Mike,' said Kildare.

'Sure they want something,' decided Mike. 'There never was a child born that didn't want something to make him thirsty or to quench it. Maybe it would be a drop of orange juice, my dear?'

'I'd like some very much,' said the girl.

'Of course you would,' said Mike, 'and a

splice of whisky to smack your lips on it?'

Kildare shook his finger at Ryan but the girl was saying: 'Yes, thank you.'

'Ah, you see?' said Mike. 'The good ones *know* what's good! And what will the young gentleman have?'

He would have the same thing; and still his eyes were asking Marguerite a question.

'And a bit of a snack of something with it?' asked Mike. 'A crumb of cheese on a cracker? Or a slice of a smoked sausage.'

'I'd like that, thank you,' she said.

'Aha, doc,' cried Mike. 'The good ones *always* know.'

... She made a slight face when she tasted the drink.

'Don't take it,' said Kildare.

'No, I'll manage it,' she said.

'But why?' insisted young Carew.

'For Mike?' suggested Kildare.

The girl smiled at him. Her eyes roved slowly from his forehead to his chin and seemed to like all that they saw.

'I'm afraid that we haven't much time,' said William Carew.

'Let's have all the time he can spare us,' said the girl. 'You have some hard things to say, haven't you, doctor?'

'You're making them easier,' he told her. 'And yet it's harder too. When I first saw you, I thought it was the usual thing, but I see that it's more than that.'

21

'I don't quite follow,' said William. 'Usual?'

'Love, and all that,' said Kildare.

'Ah, really?' said the boy, and put a cold distance instantly between them.

'But he knows, dear,' said Marguerite Paston.

'I don't like all this very much,' answered Carew. 'I'm sorry, but we have some things to do, you know.'

'You've only one thing to do,' said Kildare. 'Can't it wait just a little?'

CHAPTER THREE

WAIT A LITTLE, DEATH

'One thing?' Carew echoed. '*One* thing?' He lost a little colour and sat up straighter. He was a good athletic type, lean and hard from constant exercise. His face was drawn a bit as it is when a man is in perfect training.

The girl said nothing, but watched Kildare and Carew in turn as if the scene had little or nothing to do with her.

'You're nineteen and she's seventeen?' asked Kildare.

'That happens to be right,' admitted Carew, still drawing away from this unwelcome intimacy.

'People tell you that's too young for

22

marriage, don't they?'

'Marriage?' repeated William, lifting his eyebrows a bit.

'You went to your father to tell him that you had to get married, didn't you?'

This lifted young Carew almost out of his chair. He stared at the girl and she, still looking from one of them to the other, smiled at them both.

'Yes,' she said.

Carew settled back gingerly into his chair.

'Your father told you it was nonsense. He probably said that you should go back to school and forget all about it,' went on Kildare.

'I think you mean this kindly,' said the boy, 'but I don't see what's gained, actually, by—'

He left the final words of the sentence unuttered. His meaning was clear enough without them.

'What I want to suggest,' said Kildare, 'is that other people have to wait, and wait, and wait. Some of them manage it pretty well. Let's say that they're the cold-blooded horses. Some of the thoroughbreds won't stand it. They break away and bolt.'

He found the boy staring hard at him, silently. He went on: 'Perhaps I'm one of the cold-blooded people. But I have to wait and then keep on waiting. I don't know for how many years. But I'm managing to stand it. Does that give me the right to talk to you?'

23

A heavy silence came over them and continued for a moment. The girl suddenly had forgotten Kildare; she was closing herself into the world of William Carew.

'No, it doesn't give him the right to talk to us,' suggested the boy. He flushed and turned quickly to Kildare. 'I'm sorry,' he said. 'I don't mean to be rude.'

'It's all right. Perhaps I understand,' said Kildare. 'When there's a game, one ought to stick by the rules. But this isn't a game?'

The girl smiled a little, and still looking only at Carew she answered quietly: 'No, it's not a game.'

'So you can make up your own rules as you go,' suggested Kildare.

Neither of them answered. They remained lost in one another: not with the helpless, open stare of infatuation, but as if they were reading in one volume glorious and familiar words.

Kildare, pushed a thousand leagues away from them, drew a deep breath and continued:

'Ordinarily, a man and a woman have to work hard and wait a long time before they can be together. Perhaps that's because love itself isn't the whole thing to them.'

'What else is there that matters?' asked Carew.

'Well, there are the things that come *out* of love,' answered Kildare. 'Children, and a home, and all that, you know?'

'I know,' whispered Marguerite Paston.

'But if those things don't count so much, it leaves the man and woman free,' said Kildare.

'Free?' she repeated, lifting her head a little to greet the thought.

'Because there is nothing that can keep you apart,' said Kildare. 'It isn't a game and therefore there aren't any rules, you see.'

'But with everyone set against us,' said the girl, 'what is there that could let us be together?'

'There is that appointment you intend to keep,' said Kildare.

'What do you mean?' asked Carew, profoundly startled. 'Appointment? With whom?'

'With death,' said Kildare.

They forgot one another at last. Their frightened eyes turned on him. The girl slipped back in her chair with a white face.

'What have you done to her?' breathed Carew. 'Marguerite, we'll get out of here; we'll get away from him.'

'We can't run away—not from him!' whispered the girl.

'How did he guess?' asked Carew.

'There's not much guessing,' said Kildare. 'It's in the newspapers every day or two. They're always young. They've always found people against them. They won't meet secretly like a pair of criminals. They're proud of their love; it's the only good thing in the world. If they can't be happy and free living together, they'll be happy and free dying together.'

Carew, holding the hands of the girl, said rapidly: 'He's going to tell us what the rest of them say: that we're too young to know, that we don't understand, that life is a business, not a mere pleasure, that there is duty—'

'Hush, hush!' murmured the girl. 'He won't say any of those things. Dr Kildare, if you know what we can do, will you tell us?'

'Will you listen?' asked Kildare.

'Yes, yes—Oh, with our whole hearts we'll listen.'

Kildare closed his eyes. 'Thank God!' he said, and paused for a moment to let the tension dissolve.

'Do you see?' he heard the girl whisper.

'Yes. He's a friend!' said Carew.

Kildare looked out at them through a darkness of unhappy thought.

'Say whatever you please, and we'll listen,' said Carew, now suddenly warm and eager with friendliness. 'You can begin by telling us that we're young and silly. I hope you can prove it.'

'I don't think you're silly,' said Kildare. 'Perhaps you're the only people who are right. Perhaps the rest of us are all too old and too far away. Does that make any sense? *You* understand what I mean, don't you, Marguerite?'

'I think I do,' she said. 'Have we made you unhappy?'

'No. I can take it, all right. That word "love"—we all throw it around as if we understood it. I've wanted to marry three girls, at different times. But what have I ever known about love?

'I've been walking in the dark, compared with you two. I don't think you're foolish. I don't think lightning is foolish, either, when I see it strike. It simply never has struck me.'

'There'll come a time—' began Carew. But the girl lifted a finger and stopped him.

'Most of us are non-conductors,' said Kildare. 'The electricity won't run through us ... Foolish? No, I envy you! You make me feel that I've never been more than half alive.

'There's no love I've ever dreamed of—there's nothing on earth—that could keep me from my work. That's all I love, really—my job, and a crotchety old white-headed devil who hates disease as he hates Hell-fire...

'I envy you—but I want to keep you. That's all.'

They had forgotten their own troubles. They sat close together, hushed, watching him, and there were tears in the eyes of the girl; yet her mind kept on working.

'Are you pretending a little?' she asked.

Even Carew glanced at her in surprise.

'Do you think I am?' said Kildare.

'Just a bit?' she asked. 'To make your own life seem darker, so that what we have will be brighter, and rarer, and more worth keeping?

27

All these people love you. There's a whisper that the doc can look through people and see all their troubles as you saw ours. Oh, I think you've darkened yourself a little for our sakes.'

'Perhaps,' said Kildare. 'And perhaps I've failed.'

The boy broke out suddenly, but in a hushed voice as if he were afraid that the outer world might hear him:

'You've been great to us. You're something for us to remember. And we haven't much. But you understand how it is? Suppose I get a ding-dong job at twenty a week and put Marguerite in the dark of a little railroad flat and give her only a part of my life. That's no good.

'Sometimes being poor is all right but sometimes it's like being dirty. It would be that way with us. I'd have to give up my education and that means I'd grow up into only half a man. We'd feel as if we'd done each other in.

'There was only one hope. That was in my father and that hope we had to check out today.'

'Before you talked to him,' answered Kildare, 'did you plan what you were going to say, so that you'd be sure to get his attention?'

'You don't scheme and plan like that when you talk to your own father,' replied Carew. 'But he's hard. There's no changing him. There's not much kindness in him to make him want to understand.'

28

'You're only part of what he's fathering,' said Kildare. 'He's fathering the whole hospital; he's fathering all the schemes of the great Gillespie; he's fathering the charity wards, worrying about pay for the nurses, fees for the doctors, beds for the patients. He's kind enough to stop his whole day in order to look into a small experiment in baby feeding.

'He's a great doctor but a worried man never seems either kind or important. It's the concerns of other people that make him seem hard.'

'When you say that,' murmured Carew, 'it makes me feel that I've been a fool—a low, ungrateful fool.'

'No. You're only a little impatient,' said Kildare, 'the way your father is. But ask him for an hour of his time, plan what you're going to say to him, make everything clear; and he's going to give you whatever you ask.'

'He's not simply talking. He thinks it can be done,' said the girl.

'Why, if there's only a *ghost* of a hope, we've got to take it,' answered young Carew.

'You will?' exclaimed Kildare.

He dropped back in his chair and closed his eyes. He took a great breath.

'I thought for a while that I was lost!' he said.

CHAPTER FOUR

EMERGENCY CALL

Back in the hospital, Kildare hurried to the offices of the internist, passed through the door over which hung the brass plate which announced: *'Dr Leonard Gillespie, Hours: 12 a.m. to 12 a.m.'*

In the big waiting-room, over which Gillespie's body-servant, Conover, presided with the help of Nurse Parker, there was the usual crowd of rich men, poor men, beggar-men, and thieves who had come, some of them, half-way around the world; and the line flowed steadily in upon the diagnostician.

Kildare at once assumed, as his habit was, more than half the brunt of the work. To his eyes fell the reports and the charts of the cases as the patients were introduced, and his was the first quick attempt at diagnosis, his work to be checked by the great Gillespie.

For months he had been at it, opening every faculty wide to receive the flood of knowledge which the old man had stored up in a long life of observation, receiving a whole medical encyclopedia condensed and stingingly illustrated from the cases at hand, checked and rated for every failure of his memory—only now and then blessed with a word of praise, like a student who at the same instant is studying his courses and receiving endless final examinations in them.

The pressure, in fact, never ended as Gillespie kept driving with a ruthless hand. He made a brief pause in the flow of the line now to say:

'There was a beautiful thing here, half an hour ago, in the way of a tropical fever. You missed that, Kildare. Only a small thing, eh? But maybe it'll keep you from saving a life, one day.'

'I'm sorry, sir,' said Kildare.

'Sorry nothing!' cried Gillespie. 'You act as if you had ten years ahead of you. You act as if time didn't matter!'

'No, sir,' said Kildare, sadly, 'I know how terribly time matters.'

'Bah! Wipe that look out of your eyes!' commanded Gillespie. 'Be sentimental about other people but don't let me catch you moaning and mooning over me.'

'Did you see the doctor this morning?' asked Kildare.

'I saw him. It doesn't matter what he says. If I had six months or a whole year, what difference does it make? A man with his wits about him sometimes has a chance to do a life's work in ten minutes.

'Six months? Why, Jimmy, you and I can do as much in six months as some of the halfwits can do in six decades. But it means that we've got to work.

'I've got to have all of you, day and night, both your ears, all ten of your eyes, and all of the hundred minds that keep wandering and flying away from the subject like so many moths. That fool of a Carew ought to know that.

'Or where were you just now? Looking at the sore thumb of an elevator boy, or comforting a homesick janitor, or bandaging a pair of weak eyes, or what?'

'A boy of nineteen and a girl of seventeen very much in love—' began Kildare.

'Rot! Calves and puppies!'

'—and heading toward a suicide pact—'

'Tripe! Words, words, words—that's all.'

'—and rather happy about it,' concluded Kildare. Gillespie was hard hit by this.

'Happy about it?' he repeated.

'Yes, sir,' said Kildare.

'You mean, a great love—springtime—stardust—all that?'

'They don't care what happens, so long as it happens to them together.'

'Then it's dangerous,' declared Gillespie. 'Anything can happen! Where are they? They've got to be stopped! Kildare, don't stand there like a fool! Bring those children to me! They've got to be stopped!'

'They're stopped already,' said Kildare, smiling a little.

'*You* stopped them?'

32

'Yes, sir. They only need to get an hour of the time of a man who can solve all their problems.'

'Can they get the hour?'

'I've told them how to do it. It only needs patience.'

'That's why you're standing so much straighter, eh?'

'Yes, sir.'

'I don't blame you,' said Gillespie. 'Ordinarily we can only save lives and limbs; but the other thing—to save *that* is different, again. Ah, Kildare, there are times now and then when I think I wasn't altogether wrong in picking you—out of ten thousand!'

Later that day, Kildare was saying to Head Nurse Molly Cavendish: 'Can you tell me where Mary Lamont is?'

'What do you want her for?' said Molly Cavendish.

'For an experiment—' began Kildare.

'What kind of an experiment?' demanded the Cavendish. 'Holding hands, or what?'

'You're hard on me, Molly,' he told her.

'I'm no first name to you, either,' she said, 'at least not when I'm in uniform.' Besides, you ought to know that Nurse Lamont is off duty, now.'

'Ah, I'd forgotten her hours,' admitted Kildare. 'You don't happen to know where she went, do you?'

'How should I know and why should I tell

33

you?' snapped the Cavendish. 'I hope you understand that the internes and staff doctors are strictly forbidden to have anything to do with one another?'

'Why do we all love you when you're such a trial, Molly?' asked Kildare.

'I'll do without your love,' declared Molly Cavendish.

A big man with much jaw and very little eyes and forehead came down the corridor, his white trousers rustling from the swing of his stride. As he went by, he saluted Kildare and made an enigmatic sign.

'Tomorrow, Joe,' said Kildare, smiling.

'Thanks, doc,' said Joe.

'He was asking you,' stated Molly Cavendish, 'when you would have a beer with him in McGuire's saloon. Wasn't that it?'

'Yes,' admitted Kildare.

'Here's Dr Gillespie,' she said, 'with the world to choose from and he picks out a boy to assist him—a mere boy, and one that runs around with common guttersnipes, mere ambulance drivers like that Joe Weyman. Why do you waste time on people like Weyman?'

'He's not "people", Joe is just himself,' said Kildare.

'A hard-drinking, cheap, low, common creature. What do you owe a man like that?' demanded Cavendish hotly.

'I don't owe him my life—not quite, but almost,' said Kildare. 'But outside of that, he's as good a man as I know.'

'As good as Carew or Gillespie, perhaps?' she asked, sardonically.

'Yes. Just as good, in his own way. But speaking of Mary Lamont.'

'I'm not speaking of her.'

'Didn't she tell you where she was going?'

'Am I a letter-box or something, for you two brats to exchange messages?'

'This is an emergency, Molly.'

'What kind of an emergency?'

'I've hardly spoken to Mary for a week.'

'It's your own fault for being such a fool, then,' said the Cavendish. 'But if you were to drop in on the poor young Davisons, God help the two of them, I wouldn't be surprised if you found your Mary Lamont there.'

'What would we do without you, Molly?'

'Mind you,' she called after him, 'I'll have no more hand in these carryings-on!'

CHAPTER FIVE

LOVE IS DEAF

The Davisons lived in one room that looked onto a ventilator shaft. They could have afforded something a little better, even on eighteen dollars a week; but they had to try to save and the last of their savings had gone to the buying of the baby's crib that stood in a corner of the room. It was half decorated with windings of satin, pink and blue.

In the next corner was a kitchenette; opposite to it three chairs huddled around a floor lamp which obviously represented the living-room; and in the last corner was a couch, hardly wide enough for two. That was the bedroom.

Everyone was busy when Kildare came in. Joan Davison was laying the table, Mary Lamont worked over the gas stove, and Davison himself worked hardest of all in trying to fan the fumes of the cookery out of the window to join the other cookery smells that wafted up the shaft.

'Hi, look!' called Davison. 'Here's the young genius himself. You're getting more bumps in your forehead, Jimmy, to make room for the brains that Gillespie is pouring in.'

'Those bumps are from beating my head against the wall,' said Kildare. 'Joan, go over there and lie down. I'll finish this. I know where the things are.'

'No, I'm all right,' said the girl. 'You be a guest, Jimmy. Sit down in the living-room and be a guest.'

'That's the idea,' said Mary Lamont. 'Take her away and make her sit down. She's only in the way... But give me whatever you've brought.'

'Some ice-cream,' said Kildare, 'and a bit of

36

fresh orange juice.'

'You see?' objected Davison. 'He's always a doctor. He never forgets himself; orange juice—something alkaline—you see?'

'Finish cooking those chops, and then you're wanted,' said Kildare to Mary Lamont. 'I have to take you away.'

'Wanted? In the hospital? Really?' she asked.

'Yes,' said Kildare. 'You come here with me,' he added, taking Joan across the room.

She stretched out on the couch with a sigh. She was white and spent from the life she carried inside her.

'Stop being polite,' said Kildare. 'Close your eyes. Groan, if you feel like it.'

At this, her eyes almost closed, but she kept watching him, smiling.

'Bless you, Jimmy,' she said.

He took her hand and pressed a forefinger against her wrist.

'Don't do that,' she asked him.

'Don't bother me,' said Kildare. 'Have you been getting out in the sun?'

'Yes, whenever it comes out and shines.'

'Have you had to cry a lot?'

'Not in front of Jack.'

'Otherwise, quite a lot?'

'I'm afraid so.'

'And still a good deal of fear?'

'Not about myself; I'm not in the least afraid about myself, Jimmy.'

37

'Only what will happen to the baby, and all of you?'

'Oh, Jimmy, we only seem to be hanging to life by a spider's thread, and I'm afraid that the extra weight will break it.'

'We're going to make that thread as strong as a steel cable. You hear me?'

'I hear you. I love hearing you. Over and over.'

'Strong as a steel cable,' said Kildare.

'So nothing can break it?'

'So nothing can break it.'

'And Jack won't hate me?'

'Not too much.'

'I mean, because I'm causing him all of this trouble, and sort of dragging him down with the burden?'

'You're not dragging him down. You're only enough burden to make him stand straighter.'

'Like natives who carry packs on their heads? Oh, Jimmy, don't make me start laughing ... Do you think, really, that everything will turn out all right?'

'How can they stop Jack?' demanded Kildare. 'Gillespie noticed him today. Gillespie was talking afterwards to me about him.'

'Was he? Jimmy, was he?'

'Of course he was,' lied Kildare. 'Gillespie noticed him at once. Brains will tell. They can't stop Jack. It's only a question of getting a grip on a chance, a ghost of a chance.'

'How I love you for saying that! ... Mary, please don't go!'

'She has to. It's the hospital,' said Kildare.

Davison came over and looked down.

'Look what he's done to her already, Mary,' he said. 'A blood transfusion. How do you do it without instruments, Jimmy?'

'*I* could tell you how,' said Joan Davison.

'Go on, then,' said Davison.

'By telling lovely white lies,' said the girl, 'and by loving people so much.'

'He's a home wrecker, is that it?' asked Davison. 'I'll see them to the elevator.'

They said good night to Joan and went out into the hall. Mary Lamont walked briskly ahead toward the elevator. Kildare went slowly after her, beside Davison.

'This is a little thick, Jimmy,' said Davison. 'You come with dinner under your arm, and then you leave so there'll be more food left for us. You on your twenty a month! Don't do this again, young fellow. The next time, Joan will tumble to it. And we're not beggars yet—not quite.'

'This is no gag,' said Kildare, 'We have to get back to hospital. I got the call when I was going out.'

'You mean it, really?' asked Davison, searching the face of Kildare, but the interne supported his lie with perfect sincerity of

39

expression.

'Of course I mean it,' he said. 'I wouldn't risk anything like that. Joan's too clever. She sees through things.'

'How does she look to you?' asked Davison, anxiously.

'She's better,' Kildare lied again.

'You think so?'

'Definitely better,' said Kildare.

'She's so depressed, Jimmy. Break your heart to see how she's always fighting off the blues and cheering up for my sake.'

'She's a real one, all right,' said Kildare. 'By the way, Gillespie is talking about you. Maybe we can wangle something.'

'Is he talking?' asked Davison, eagerly. 'Listen, Jimmy, whoever helps me now, Jimmy—till I can see the child born and Joan well and strong ... But a girl in that shape—you know, they live on hope and happiness more than on food. That's why you're so good for her. Come in often, will you?'

'Of course. What's specially hard on you just now, Jack?'

'Nothing. There's nothing specially wrong. Just things in general.'

'There's something particularly bad. What is it? What are you breaking your heart about?'

'You relentless mind-reader! But there's nothing you could help about. No use telling you.'

'There's always a use in telling it. It gets it

partly off your chest. Tell me what's up.'

'Something that only money can cure. I took her to see Doctor Langsley. You know him?'

'He's one of the tops,' agreed Kildare. 'What did he say about Joan?'

'He says she needs a change of air. Plenty of red meat and a different climate. A month in Florida, for instance.

'A month in Florida,' repeated Davison. 'A week in heaven—a thousand dollars—it doesn't matter; one thing is as far away as the other. Jimmy, a woman's a fool if she marries a poor man. And there ought to be a law against doctors marrying.'

'She doesn't need Florida. She needs a dash more hope; and we're going to find it for her,' said Kildare.

He was silent, afterward, as the elevator carried him and Mary clanking down to the street level. It was one of those old, hydraulic crates and it gave a prison voice of complaint and a prison atmosphere to the tenement.

When they were out on the street, Mary Lamont stopped to look up and down.

'Which way?' she asked.

'What makes you know it's not the hospital?' he asked.

'Because I'm beginning to know you quite well. At least, I know when you're lying.'

'I've got a job for you, but it's not in the hospital.'

'All right, whom do I have to mother now?'

'You're looking tops,' said Kildare. 'I like that red doowhickus in your hat.'

'That's just in order to pretend that this is Christmas. Besides, you like red.'

'I never said so.'

'No, but you've looked it. You're always looking and saying things without words. What's the new job?'

'How tired are you?'

'I still can walk and talk.'

'Take my arm.'

'All right. You don't like this, usually.'

'I like it tonight.'

'Because you're feeling pretty far away from me?'

'Don't talk like that.'

'Oh, but you're pretty distant. You wonder what you're doing walking along with this girl. Who is she? What does she mean?'

'Quit it, Mary.'

'She's the same girl, all right. These are the same old shoes, the same old gloves, the same three-year-old coat.'

He looked straight ahead, forgetting her. 'I want you to go see Marguerite Paston,' he said.

'Ah, that sweet, sweet thing?'

'Yes. You were right about her. She's a charm. Here's her address.'

'That's good. I'll be glad to see her. What's it all about?'

'I can't tell you the details.'

'Honour-bound, and all that?'

'Yes.'

'You are *such* an honourable fool, Jimmy, darling.'

'She's dangerously unhappy. That's all you really need to know.'

'Dangerously?'

'Sometimes love is a dangerous nerve condition,' said Kildare.

'I can almost *hate* you sometimes, Jimmy. Do you always have to be a doctor?'

'And if you'll remember Juliet, and Sarah Churchill, and Héloïse...'

'You mean, till-death-do-us-part, and all that?'

'That's the idea. You're going to go and see this girl and talk to her. You've got to have a theme, but better than anything I can give you is what you'll find in her.'

'Tell me what. Give me an idea.'

'The point is that you'll have to find your own theme, out of her. She needs watching, Mary.'

'I'll watch her, then. I knew that you'd want me to be a mother, again. She's dangerously unhappy?'

'She's sure that it's only a step from earth to heaven. You see?'

'I see. That's pretty bad, Jimmy.'

'I think that I've got her on the right path—hopeful, and all that. But I'm not sure. You're the one who has to make sure for me.'

'How do I lead off?'

'She's a little in need of a tonic. I asked you to take one over to her. Buy some junk in a drugstore.'

'Won't she see through that?'

'She doesn't see through crooked things. She understands all of the good and none of the evil.'

'All right. And then what?'

'Then you tell her how much everybody loves her. How you love her and how I do.'

'You? No, no, Jimmy. I don't want to exaggerate. You have compassion, but you don't love.'

'Oh, don't I?'

'Not a whack. You're fuller of compassion than a loaf is full of dough and air-holes. But love is a different matter.'

'If that's true, then I'm sorry,' he said.

'In another minute,' she said, 'you'll take compassion on me, too. You'll cut yourself out of my life and my heart and give me a chance to get a better man. That's the way you'll take compassion, so I'd better shut up . . .

'I don't know why I talk this way. It must be the Christmas that's in the air. It's gone to my head . . .

'I don't want to be satirical, Jimmy. I'm loving you all the while I'm sticking pins in you. But women are such idiotic creatures! . . . Why are you stopping here?'

'I want you to finish . . . And then this is the address of Marguerite.'

44

'I'm to finish my tirade, first?'

He was silent.

'Well, you finish it for me, will you?' she asked. 'There's not too much light, is there?'

He took her in his arms and kissed her.

CHAPTER SIX

HAIL—AND FAREWELL!

More than a week later—snatching an interruption in the steady stream through his office—the great Gillespie was saying: 'What do you think of his chances?'

'About six weeks,' said Kildare.

'Who was I talking about?'

'The fourth man before the last one. The coronary case.'

'Six weeks? Six months, rather, if he watches himself.'

'He won't watch himself, sir.'

'No,' said Gillespie, sadly, 'he won't watch himself. Next patient! ... No, hold it a minute! How's that Scotch baby doing?'

'Pete Douglas? Not so well, sir.'

'I'm sorry. We ought to know more about that formula and its variations, Jimmy. Why don't we hear from your father?'

'Perhaps he's having a Christmas rush;

people getting ready for the holidays, you know.'

'Do they do that out in Dartford?'

'Yes, they're afraid of the cider but they know that they won't keep away from it. Still, it's pretty queer that he hasn't mailed us the notes.'

'What's happening tomorrow?'

'The Norwegian gets the operation.'

'What else?'

'There's the hyperthyroid, also.'

'What else?'

'You've promised me a bit of a talk on endocarditis.'

'What else?'

'I don't recall anything particularly.'

'What about Christmas itself?'

'There's that, of course.'

'Isn't that an event in your life?'

'Naturally, sir.'

'Are you going home?'

'I think I should watch that hyperthyroid, sir.'

'Forget the hyperthyroid. Ring your house this moment and find out why your father hasn't sent in that material about the feeding formula.'

'Yes, sir, as soon as this next case of thrombosis—'

'Never mind the next case. The first case is always the home case. Never forget that. Take the phone in the other room ... Next patient!'

Kildare went into the second office where his own desk stood and where Mary Lamont was making rapid notations on cards three by five, for a file. As he settled himself to telephone, she came over and put her head down beside his.

'Yes?' asked Kildare, looking up.

'Nothing,' she said, and turned away.

'Come back, Mary,' he called.

'Yes, doctor?' she answered, showing him a cold face.

'I'm sorry,' he said.

'It's quite all right,' she said.

He sighed and shrugged his shoulders. After a moment he rang the Dartford number. His mother answered.

'It's almost merry Christmas,' said Kildare.

'Are you coming, Jimmy? Are you going to be able to make it?' she asked eagerly.

'There's a hyperthyroid that I've got to watch,' he said. 'I'm terribly sorry.'

'Oh, I know, I know. I've spent most of my life learning that a doctor has to be a doctor, but somehow I keep forgetting.'

'Is father there?'

'Your father? No, Jimmy—no, he's not here.'

'You say that in a queer way.'

'I've just a touch of cold, dear. That's all.'

'No, there's something wrong, isn't there?'

'No, Jimmy. No, no, there's nothing wrong at all.'

He reflected for an instant on the slight

tremor that had come into her voice and left it again, a faint resonance like the music of grief.

He remembered, sadly, that she was growing old and what he had heard might be merely the weakness of increasing age; or perhaps she was unhappy because he was not coming home for Christmas; or it might be any of those thousand shadows which drift across the minds of women, imperceptible to the grosser eyes of men.

He began to probe a bit, carefully.

'Has father told you about an experiment we're doing for him?' he asked.

'No, dear.'

'What? Not a word?'

'I'm afraid not, Jimmy.'

'About the baby formula we're trying out here?'

'Oh, yes. About that, yes—I think so.'

Kildare frowned as he listened.

'He was going to send us in the rest of his notes. Will you ask him about them?'

'Good-bye—and merry Christmas...'

He was still frowning when he went back into the other office and Gillespie said instantly: 'What's wrong now? Aren't those notes in the mail?'

'No,' said Kildare. 'My father was a bit excited—just quietly a bit excited—over the idea that we might be able to publish his work. Wouldn't you have said so?'

'Of course. He was as happy as a boy.'

'Then he couldn't help talking about it to mother. He couldn't help making a rather big thing out of it, could he?'

'Why, he couldn't be sure that things are happening unless they're in her mind as well as his own,' declared Gillespie. 'He doesn't know the day has started until she says the sun is up. He can't taste the news, even, unless he reads her the headlines.'

Kildare did not smile.

'Well,' he said, 'she seems hardly to know whether or not she's heard about the experiment.'

'Next patient, sir?' Conover was saying at the door.

'Hold up the line!' commanded Gillespie. 'Jimmy, what the devil is wrong out there in Dartford?'

'She's unhappy but she won't tell me what's going on. I don't suppose it can be important.'

'Why couldn't it be important? If she were two steps away from dying, she wouldn't tell you. She'd be afraid of stealing some of your time. Those two old fools are so bound on carrying their own burdens that they'd drown in a quicksand rather than ask you to stretch out your hand to them.'

'I think they would,' agreed Kildare, slowly.

'Anything in her way of speaking?'

'There was one tremor, I thought—but only one.'

'How could there be more than one?'

demanded Gillespie. 'She'll never show weakness. She's all bulldog. She reminds me of a young interne I know: an idiot who's always searching out lost causes and locking his jaws on them, do or die...

'What are you going to do about this?'

'If it weren't for the hyperthyroid,' said Kildare, 'I'd go home, with your permission, sir.'

'Permission? Permission?' exclaimed the fierce old man. 'I'll go out to Dartford *with* you. I haven't looked a real Christmas turkey in the face for thirty years.

'And if those people are in trouble, there's no hyperthyroid, there's no hospital, there's nothing else in the world that's worth a thought—for twenty-four hours!'

It was about this time that Marguerite Paston and young Carew went into the office of his father confidently, their heads high; and a half hour later they came out again with pale, set faces.

They walked slowly, with searching, wide eyes, as if they were moving through the dark. When they came out into the long hall, young William Carew said: 'Well, we had the extra days and the hope; but even Kildare would agree with us now.'

'I think he would,' said the girl.

'There's only one thing left. You still feel that?'

'What else is there?' she asked.

50

They looked not at one another but straight down the length of the hall, as white, as immaculate as eternity.

'We ought to see Doctor Kildare and say good-bye,' said Carew.

'No,' the girl answered. 'It wouldn't be right.'

'He'd never try to stop us. He understands. It's queer, isn't it? Two or three billion people in the world, and only one of them understands.'

'But it would be terrible pain to him. He wouldn't try to stop us, but I know how his face would look.'

'It couldn't mean so much; we're hardly more than strangers to him.'

'We're more than that. He understands trouble the moment he sees it and it hurts him.'

'Maybe you're right, but I think that I've got to say good-bye to him, face to face; otherwise, somehow, it would be like sneaking out.'

'I think you're right,' she agreed.

That was why they went down to the office of Gillespie. People still were trailing disconsolately out of the big waiting-room and Conover gave young Carew the bad news that Kildare and Gillespie both had left the hospital.

'We'll leave a note for him,' said William Carew. 'You write it, Marguerite. You know how to make words say something.'

And she wrote:

DEAR DOCTOR KILDARE:

Everything you said to us was kind and wise, but when we went to him it was like talking to a face of stone. Perhaps he's right in calling us fools, because there may be no place for people like us. We feel a sort of strength but not for the kind of life we would have to follow; so we're taking the other way. We wanted to see you, first, because in the whole world you're the only one who will understand.

MARGUERITE PASTON
WILLIAM CAREW

When they both had signed it, Carew gave the envelope to Conover. He took it back to Kildare's office and gave it to Mary Lamont.

'It ain't from patients. It's personal,' said Conover.

'Oh, personal?' murmured the nurse, and tossed the letter carelessly aside.

By that time Marguerite Paston and young Carew were once more out in the street. A wind was sliding down off the northern shoulders of the world, bringing with it a level-driven spray of snow that cut off the breath sharply.

They turned from the weight of the storm and looked back down the street of ten thousand windows, like a double row of tall desks in which so many lives had been pigeon-holed forever.

52

CHAPTER SEVEN

SO THIS IS CHRISTMAS!

The storm which sang so high over Manhattan was bringing down on Dartford such a fall of snow that the cottages were blinded and isolated each in its own horizon like a ship on a lonely sea.

When the door opened on the kitchen of Mrs Stephen Kildare the noise of the wind entered with a hollow roar and was shut out suddenly again like the roar of a fast train which comes and passes in an instant.

Kildare, his coat spotted with snow, kissed his mother and took a breath of the Christmas fragrance of evergreen decorations together with the steaming spicery of plum puddings and mince pies and pungent stuffings and the rich odour of roasting meat.

Steam rose from the old-fashioned range to frost on the windows and fog the air so that he saw only one person in the room.

'You're not home for Christmas, Jimmy,' she was crying to him. 'You're *not* home for Christmas, after all.'

'I'm nothing,' said Kildare. 'I'm only an interne. Wait till you see the surprise I've brought for you. You and father get ready at the front door. I'm bringing my present in that way!'

'But, Jimmy—' she began; and found herself speaking to emptiness as he disappeared into the white uproar of the storm again.

She turned to Beatrice Raymond, who was in a corner peeling thin-skinned Florida oranges; she was half invisible in the dim blue of an old apron.

'Think of him not seeing *you*,' said Mrs Kildare. 'Take off that apron, my dear, and we'll go to the front door.'

'No, I'll stay here,' said Beatrice.

'Are you hurt, child?'

'No, not very much.'

'Darling, you know how Jimmy is—just half blind—'

'I know he is,' said Beatrice, managing to smile a little. 'Half blind until he wants to see something.'

'Don't say that, Beatrice. Don't, please, take it this way.'

'It's all right; that other business is over and done with.'

'It isn't, though. Beatrice, take off that wretched apron. I want him to see you in that sweet dress.'

'No, he doesn't look at dresses. I'll stay right here, please.'

Mrs Kildare could not stay to argue. A noise at the front door sent her flying and she arrived in time to see the door thrust open in front of the wheel-chair of the great Gillespie with Big

Joe Weyman pushing him forward.

The doctor tossed his hat ahead of him and as the wind knocked his hair into a white confusion he called: 'There's my hat in the ring, woman. I'll out-eat, out-drink, and out-talk the best man in your house.

'Where's that husband of yours? I've been waiting thirty years for a Christmas like this and now I'm going to show him what a real man can do to it.'

'Stephen will be here in just a moment,' she said as Kildare came in last and shut the door. 'He'll surely be back soon.'

'Well, if we can't have him, we'll have the kitchen,' declared Gillespie. 'Let me come back there into your operating room, will you?'

'Mother, you know my friend Weyman?' asked Kildare. 'We stole him from the hospital to drive us out here.'

'Joe and I know all about each other,' she answered, 'because we know about *you*, Jimmy.'

'Where's father?' asked Kildare.

'He'll be here any time,' she said, trying to escape.

He touched her arm and kept her, in the meantime waving Weyman and the wheelchair forward.

'Where's Father?' he repeated.

'He's out and busy. But he'll be back...'

She kept smiling up at him while Kildare studied her solemnly. From the kitchen they heard Gillespie roaring:

55

'Come out from the corner there, you. You're what's going to make this Christmas merry for me. Tell me your name—and isn't there any mistletoe in this house?'

'There's trouble about father,' Kildare was insisting. 'It was in your voice in the telephone. Tell me what's wrong.'

'There's nothing wrong ... We can't leave Doctor Gillespie alone in there. Good heavens, Jimmy, think of such a man in our little house!'

'It's no good dodging,' declared Kildare. 'What's happening?'

She closed her eyes and put a hand on the arm of Kildare to steady herself. She said: 'Medwick. The last doctor's gone from that town and your father's trying to take care of all the sick.'

'That would kill any one man,' said Kildare. She was silent as she nodded.

'When was he last home?' asked Kildare.

'Yesterday morning. I've begged and I've prayed to him, Jimmy. But he says that doctors take an oath ... And now I've told you and he'll never forgive me for putting the worry on you!'

'Hush, hush!' commanded Kildare. 'Since yesterday morning he hasn't been here. That means he hasn't slept. I'm going to Medwick now.'

'And leave Doctor Gillespie? Your father would never forgive—'

'Would we ever forgive ourselves?' asked

Kildare. 'That's what's important. I'm starting for Medwick now ... Don't let Weyman sit too near the whisky bottle...'

'Why argue with him?' asked Gillespie, when Mrs Kildare still protested against the departure of her son for the town of Medwick. 'We don't argue with him in the hospital. If you try to hold him, he breaks down the wall and knocks a hole in the roof.'

So Kildare departed in the Raymond automobile and Gillespie set himself to bringing a little more cheer into the household, until the last gleam of daylight was gone from behind the storm; and then the winter night came in, suddenly still and clear, and yet neither Jimmy nor his father appeared.

Even in spite of Gillespie's determined cheerfulness, a silence kept invading the Kildare house, spreading coldly, while they looked wide-eyed at one another. In weather such as that day, any sort of accident could have happened along the road; and there was not even a telephone call.

'It's my turn to go,' said Gillespie. 'This is a sort of fairy story. The oldest son goes out to the enchanted castle and doesn't come back. The second son goes and never returns. At last the youngest son sharpens his sword, tightens his belt, and takes the road toward the giant. That's the cue for young Gillespie.

'Weyman, get me out into that car. We're going to Medwick!'

Mrs Kildare and Beatrice Raymond went out beside the wheel-chair to the automobile. It was so cold that even the wind was frozen. There was not a breath of it.

Gillespie was bundled into the car, his wheel-chair collapsed and put in the luggage compartment, and Weyman took his place behind the wheel.

'Men have the easy jobs,' said Gillespie. 'They go out and discover the news, but women have to stay at home and wait for it.

'I know what's going on in your head, madame. But what about the "gone" look of Beatrice? You're not worrying so much about two old men. It's Jimmy who's making you hold your breath, isn't it?'

'We grew up together, you know,' she said. She managed to laugh. 'But then Dartford turned out to be too small, you know.'

'Maybe it'll seem big again to him, some day,' said Gillespie. 'I'll be back in an hour or two with a whole collection of Kildares.'

Weyman, as he sent the car out of the small town, was saying: 'This Doc Kildare. Quiet and all—but they know when he's around, don't they?'

'You mean, the women know?' asked Gillespie.

'That's right, sir.'

'I can't tell what they know or when they know it,' said Gillespie. 'When I'm with women, Joe, I talk louder but I know less.

58

'Drive like hell. I want to get to Medwick. I've got an idea that we've bad news for Christmas ahead of us.'

So Weyman drove. Where the wind had scoured the road, it was as slippery as greased marble and the rest of the way they sent out a fanning cloud of snow-dust behind them until they crossed the state line into Medwick.

It was not very much larger than Dartford, though the factories gave it an air of greater and more gloomy significance. The moon which shone now out of the clear sky showed Gillespie the long, low buildings of glass and brick and steel, with a thousand panes knocked in and one broken-backed roof.

The town itself was demure rows of cottages set back behind lawns and overstretched by huge elm trees which lined the streets.

Gillespie had Weyman stop at a filling station. They took ten gallons of gasoline and had a chance to talk with the attendant as he scraped the frost from the windshield.

'It's got a good hillside position, this town,' said Gillespie. 'Ought to be healthy.'

'Why, Medwick is one of the healthiest towns in the world,' said the native. 'When we get the marshes drained, down there, we'll be clean rid of the fever. We're so healthy around here that I'll tell you something: We been getting along without a doctor, even!'

He beamed widely.

'That's good for the town but bad for me,'

59

said Gillespie. 'I've got a sore throat that I hoped I could get painted up right here.'

'Come to think of it,' said the attendant, 'there might be a doctor down in the Lancey house just now. I've heard there's somebody sick down there. Turn left three blocks down and it's the second house on the right-hand side.'

The Lancey house was like the rest of the cottages. Weyman rang at the front door and it was opened at once by a woman who carried a baby wrapped in a shawl.

'Doctor Kildare here?' asked Weyman.

'I don't know the name, but there's two doctors here. One of 'em is too young to amount to much. Come on in and wait for your turn. They're working out in the kitchen.'

Weyman took the news back to Gillespie.

'We'll take 'em in the flank and rear,' said Gillespie. 'Wheel me around to the kitchen door, Joe.'

Weyman pulled out the chair, set it up, and pushed the doctor into the backyard. Through a window from which the frost was half thawed, they looked in on a woman stretched out on two deal tables, put end to end.

The elder Kildare handled the anaesthetic; his son worked at an abdominal operation on the white-robed figure.

'Look at those hands, Weyman!' said Gillespie. 'Look at the way he's tying off, faster than a woman could crochet. Only one half-

60

power electric light to see by, but hands like those can find their way in the dark.

'Get me in there! That old Kildare is blue in the face. He's as like as not to drop dead any minute!'

The door was unlocked. Weyman wheeled in the chair but the two doctors were too intent on their work to look up until Gillespie said:

'Trying to keep your Christmas all to yourselves? Go lie down on the floor before you *fall* down, Steve ... Go on and do what I tell you; you're dropping now.

'I'll take charge of that anaesthetic; push me around to the head of the table.'

'Can you manage all right?' asked old Kildare. 'It's a brittle pulse. I don't like her heart at all ... And I'll just take your advice for a moment.'

He slumped down on the floor in a corner, so spent that his head knocked heavily on the boards. He threw out his arms wide and lay like a cross, his eyes shut, his breathing slow and audible.

Gillespie and young Kildare had not spoken. Now their eyes crossed with glances of intent understanding.

'He's had a week of it, day and night,' murmured Kildare.

'Get my medical kit out of the car, Joe,' directed Gillespie; the stethoscope he had taken from old Kildare now pressed over the heart of the patient.

61

'How is she holding?' asked Kildare, still rapidly at work inside the yawning incision.

Gillespie was silent. Kildare looked up with a single incisive glance, set his jaw hard, and continued his work.

'She'll just last it out,' announced Gillespie, finally.

'Thank God for that!' breathed Kildare.

Gillespie reached out with a handkerchief and swabbed the dripping forehead of Kildare. In both hands Kildare lifted out a red mass and dropped it into a garbage can. His swift fingers began to close the wound.

'She's too young to have a heart like this,' said Gillespie. 'What's wrong with her?'

'Malnutrition, sir.'

'Are they going hungry in this town?'

'No, sir. Plenty to eat, but sometimes the wrong things.'

A faint sound of complaint came from the corner of the room. Far lost in the sleep of exhaustion, old Kildare was groaning with every breath.

The automatic hands of the son went swiftly on; his mind was left free for the explanation.

'A year ago the factories closed. They moved South. The doctors scattered. There wasn't any money left to pay them. Only old Doctor Brewster remained. He couldn't stand twenty hours a day. Whisky didn't help him—much. He died a week ago. And father took over.'

'This town and Dartford too?'

'Yes, sir.'

'*All* the Kildares are fools,' said Gillespie. 'If they have to play Santa Claus, why don't they wear masks and beards and fat bellies so the rest of us can tell what they are? ... What's that door doing, leaning against the wall?'

'That's our stretcher, sir ... This one is ready for it now. Weyman, give me a hand?'

'All right, doc. Where to?'

'There's a couch in the hall upstairs. All the other beds are filled.'

'What are you doing for nurses?' asked Gillespie.

'Women of the town,' said Kildare. 'Will you look into the living-room, sir? It's full of people who need help. For a year they've been too poor to pay for a doctor and too proud to take charity.'

'What have they been paying your father, then?'

'Why, he's different,' explained Kildare. 'People don't mind taking what he's able to give.'

'Yeah, because he's like you, doc,' broke in Weyman. 'And you always seem like one of the family.'

'Bah!' said Gillespie. 'It's all maudlin rot. What people get for nothing is poison to their souls ... Let me have a look at your waiting-room!'

He found there twenty of the villagers, from an old man huddled on the floor with both

63

arms wrapped around a tortured body, to a white-faced, staring girl of fifteen; and not fewer than five mothers with infants in their arms.

Only the Medwick people who were desperate, it seemed, would take charity to relieve their pain.

Old Gillespie, instantly, had one of the children stretched in his lap, commencing an examination.

CHAPTER EIGHT

THREE AGAINST DEATH

Rain came during the night, thawing and sliding the snow from the roofs of Medwick, running from a thousand faucets, as it were, off every corner.

The frost dissolved on the windows to oily smears and the compacted snow on the streets rotted to a yellow mush.

Late the next morning, still in the Lancey house, still in the kitchen, the two Kildares sat around the stove drinking black coffee. Doctor Stephen steadied his cup with both of his shaking hands.

Gillespie said: 'Diagnosing a case off-hand, Stephen, what would you say if you saw a man with blue pouches under his eyes, his face a

64

bluish-white, trembling voice, uncertain gestures, an expression of frowning, concentration, no appetite, nervous tension around his mouth, blue veins apparent in the forehead?'

'It suggests a kidney condition, perhaps,' said old Kildare, 'or perhaps—'

He jerked up his head and listened. The sick wail of a baby had been coming constantly from an upper room in the Lancey house. It seemed to have broken in on the old man's attention with fresh force.

'That may be simply stomach ache, after all,' he suggested.

'Never mind the baby. Go back to the description I've just given you. Kidney condition, you say?'

'Well, not necessarily,' answered Stephen Kildare.

'Simple exhaustion after a prolonged strain, perhaps.'

'Dangerous, would you say?' asked Gillespie.

'Wouldn't that depend upon the age and the physical resistance of the patient, Leonard?'

'Suppose a patient advanced in years?' said Gillespie. 'A patient habitually overworked and still driven by his conscience. What would you prescribe?'

'Bed rest,' said old Kildare. 'Rather indefinite bed rest, I think, together with sedatives and . . .'

'Exactly!' agreed Gillespie. 'And by the way, what do you think of the fools who imperil themselves and their families and the affections of their friends because of a crackpot, silly devotion to what they think is their duty?'

'Ah, there's a point I've often tried to make,' said old Kildare. 'There are too many nerves in the American machine. It worries itself to death. It refuses to wait till tomorrow. It tries to do everything today. Nerve strain is rotting away the strength of the American man, Leonard!'

'Then why don't you go home and get to bed—for an indefinite period, or until a competent physician tells you that you safely may get up?'

The old doctor, who saw that he was fairly trapped, smiled and tried to shrug the suggestion away; but the other two were not amused. They stared at him with grimly accusing eyes.

'It's exactly what I shall do,' said Stephen Kildare, at last, 'as soon as the Medwick condition is a little improved.'

'The confoundest nonsense I ever heard of!' answered Gillespie. 'You're trying to carry the entire burden on your shoulders whereas there's enough work here in Medwick, continually, not for one old practitioner, but for five or six young ones.'

Old Kildare, with a covert wink, made to Gillespie a gesture which implored secrecy, and at the same time indicated his son.

'Why should I shut up because Jimmy is listening to me?' demanded Gillespie. 'You're afraid that before long he'll make Medwick one of his lost causes and stick to it like a bulldog and let his hospital work and future go hang?'

'Why, Stephen, he's decided to do that already, because he's his father's son and believes that the life and future happiness of one doctor are nothing compared to the health and happiness of a whole community.

'Now, Stephen, will you listen to reason?'

Old Kildare groaned: 'I'll do whatever you say, Leonard. I'll withdraw—as soon as the condition here is a little better.'

'Suppose we get half a dozen young doctors out here with plenty of brains and no practices?' demanded Gillespie.

'Very good—in almost any other part of the country,' said Stephen Kildare. 'But this is New England, Leonard. This is a highly respectable and intensely conservative community. The men of Medwick are the same blood that has led the whole nation in the great emergencies. I can't tell how they would welcome a group of young, of very young and inexperienced—'

'Wouldn't they be accepted with your recommendation behind them?' asked Gillespie.

'Nothing like that would be accepted

without the backing of Winslow. He's the chief citizen and the leader of the community.'

'Get him here, then!' commanded Gillespie.

'I could take you to his office in his bank,' said Kildare.

'Ah, the rich man, is he?'

'No, not rich. He has a small fortune that he made out of the town, and he's putting his money back into Medwick trying to stave off depression until the place gets on its feet again.

'The people follow him because Medwick is his religion and he's the chief priest of the cult. He's a father to every poor man in the district—a rather irascible father, recently, a sort of benevolent tyrant as he sees his town go downhill.'

'Let him be whatever he is,' said Gillespie, 'but get him in here to listen to that baby's crying.'

Experts in torment tell us that there is in nature nothing more heart-rending than the shriek of the rabbit when the teeth of the greyhound close on it or, at the other end of the scale, the scream of a tortured horse, when a voice comes to the mute beast as it dies.

But to rouse up even the most callous of men and put him into violent action, there is nothing to compare with the brainless, whining, insistent cry of an infant.

Geoffrey Winslow, when he came into the Lancey house with old Stephen Kildare, could not keep from turning his head toward the sound of the baby's wailing.

He was sixty and very grey; but from a distance he was so straight-standing and carried his head with such an air of command that he seemed still in the full of his vigour.

Only when he came nearer could it be seen how time had worn him, just as a green hill may turn out to have a face covered with the fine lines and gullies of erosion. Around his mouth there were signs of the same nervous tension which Gillespie had pointed out in Stephen Kildare.

They passed through the living-room, where a dozen people were still gathered in spite of the long work which the three doctors had been carrying on. Everyone stood up and smiled at the great man of the town. There was just a touch of fear in their eyes, however.

But he spoke to them one by one, quickly, shaking hands and wishing them a merry Christmas, before he accompanied Stephen Kildare back into the kitchen, which still served as a consulting-room.

Gillespie was there, saying to an unhappy woman: 'Even a very young doctor may be right, Mrs Jasper. Young Doctor Kildare noticed among other things a slight malformation of the legs of your son, and a peculiar squareness in the head.

'Those are signs of rickets, Mrs Jasper, and the thing for you to do is to feed your boy exactly the diet which Dr Kildare suggests to you.'

'He only gave my Tommy one look!' complained Mrs Jasper. 'It doesn't seem right that a youngster like that doctor could know so much in just one look.'

Gillespie explained with unusual calm: 'There are a great many older doctors who cannot see as much in a year as young Dr Kildare can see in a glance. Musicians and poets are born, not made, Mrs Jasper, and so are diagnosticians. They look deeper than the skin; they have X-ray eyes. So you just run along and do what he told you.'

'I'll do it,' said Mrs Jasper, shaking her head, 'but just the same it don't seem hardly right.'

As she went out, Kildare was saying: 'This is Doctor Gillespie, of whom I've told you; Doctor Gillespie, this our leading citizen of Medwick, Mr Winslow... My son doesn't seem to be here.'

'He's up working on that crying baby,' said Gillespie.

'I should think that the child's mother might quiet it,' suggested Geoffrey Winslow.

'She's tried,' said Gillespie. 'Now, Mr Winslow, has my friend, Doctor Kildare, told you what we want to speak about?'

'I don't want to talk out of turn,' answered the banker. 'I'm not a medical man and therefore my medical opinions aren't worth much; but I've seen a bit of life and people and I can't say that I'd put much trust in a crew of

70

youngsters who haven't had the school of real experience. I don't think the town would, either.'

'No experience?' echoed Gillespie. 'The men we have in mind are fellows who have done distinguished work for four years in their medical schools; then they've had, each of them, two years of hard work in hospitals; and after that some of them have assisted specialists for a still longer time.

'But when they came to hang out their shingles they found that there were a good many people in the world who felt like you, Mr Winslow—that only age could be trusted.

'But haven't you noticed that age sometimes forgets what young men still remember? Recently, have you ever happened to glance into the school algebra that you once knew by heart? Dead stuff to you now, isn't it?'

'That's true,' admitted Winslow, grudgingly. 'But medicine handles matters of life and death.'

'So do generals in a time of war,' answered Gillespie. 'In time of peace, greyheads lead our armies. In time of war they go into the junk heap. Right through history, the greatest battles are won by young, new leaders.'

There was a point to this remark that Winslow did not care to answer at once. He said: 'A house full of sick people—a baby crying—it's almost as if the stage had been set to persuade me.'

71

'But notice that the baby isn't crying any longer,' said Gillespie. 'That very young doctor, Kildare, has found some way to ease it, probably to cure it of pain and sickness at the same time.'

'True,' said Winslow, discovering with surprise that the painful cry no longer was stabbing into his brain. 'After all, this lad is *your* son, Dr Kildare.'

'He's no better than the other men we'd bring out to Medwick,' said Stephen Kildare.

'Not a whit better; younger, less experienced, in fact,' insisted Gillespie.

Winslow gave him a sour look. He half turned and faced old Kildare.

'Perhaps, perhaps,' he said, 'but people around here put their trust in old friends, true friends—like you! Now, if you give your blessing to the proposition, Doctor Kildare, I might be able, in all conscience, to recommend these young men to Medwick. Do you put yourself behind them?'

'With my whole heart!'

CHAPTER NINE

SIX LONG SHOTS

Young Dr Kildare, back at the hospital with a mission before him, nevertheless paused to tear off his clothes and take a two-minute shower.

Then hurrying to his office he threw himself face down upon the couch and said across his shoulder to the nurse: 'Wake me up in half an hour, Mary.'

'What is it, Jimmy?' she asked.

'Hell's popping,' he answered, closed his eyes, and was instantly asleep. His loosened muscles let his arm slide over the edge of the couch. His hand fell with a rap against the floor but he was not roused.

Mary Lamont replaced the arm. She sat down beside him and began to massage the corrugated, congested muscles at the base of the skull and down the neck.

Kildare gave a great, sighing exhalation of perfect relief and fell into a sounder sleep.

Her hands still were at work when the half hour ended. She studied her wrist-watch for a moment, then shook his arm and spoke to him. No stir of answer came from Kildare. She leaned and kissed him.

'All right,' said Kildare, and sat up. He spilled back against a cushion and the wall.

'Wake me up,' he said.

She took a wet towel and wiped his face, his throat.

'That'll do,' said Kildare.

He stood up, stretched, yawned on tiptoe, and settled back on his heels.

'Anything happening?' he asked.

'Christmas, Jimmy,' she said. 'And here's

73

something I thought might be useful to you when you're...'

'Nice of you, Mary,' he said, and took the white parcel in his hands. He started to untie the red ribbon. The knot pulled hard.

'I'll undo it, darling,' she said.

He kept his hands on the parcel, not hearing her. His blind fingers went on fumbling.

'Anything I need to know?' he asked.

'Nothing. Except a personal message for you.'

She picked up the letter of Marguerite Paston and young Carew.

'I'll look at it later,' said Kildare. 'Personal? I'm not a person. I'm just a doctor.'

'Doctors aren't people?' she asked, trying to smile.

'Of course not,' said Kildare, without smiling.

'Of course not,' she agreed.

'Where does Midge Whalen live?'

'Seventy-two, Morris Place.'

'Ben Connor?'

'One forty-three B West Seventieth.'

'Sammy Darnell?'

'Eleven eighty-three Linden Avenue, Flatbush.'

'Sid Garfield?'

'That must be the wrong name,' said Mary Lamont.

'Wrong?'

'He's not one of your addresses. I don't think he is.'

'Sid Garfield? The dentist?'

'You don't know dentists also, do you, dear?'

'Of course I know them.'

Here the instinctive wits in his surgeon's fingers untied the knot and stripped the red ribbon from the package. He went on:

'That's where half the trouble gets into the body: the mouth, you know. And that's where the dentist comes in. You think of some of the old-time boys who were chiefly mechanics. Finer mechanics than watch-makers, but not much more important.

'The new crowd are different. They have to be mechanics, internists, surgeons, doctors, all in one. They are working all the time at the sources.'

'Yes, dear.'

'You're not interested?'

'Oh, yes, Jimmy! But don't you want to see . . .'

She pointed at the unopened parcel.

'Write down those addresses while I get my coat on.'

She picked up a pad and pencil and began to write as he hurried into his coat.

'What is it, Jimmy? What's the lost cause this time?'

'A whole town full of the best people you ever saw. All made of oak and iron like old

75

ships. Finest people in the world—and the most pig-headed.

'No doctor there for a year. A big back-log of cases crying out for treatment; and a lot of New England pride to keep them away from a charity clinic; maybe a hundred lives to save; maybe a thousand that need straightening...'

'Beautiful, Jimmy, isn't it?' she asked.

Kildare, his eyes on the ceiling, hardly heard her.

'If I had five pairs of hands and five brains behind them—and I'm going to get the hands and the brains right now. Good-bye!'

She picked up the white parcel.

'Good-bye, Jimmy,' she said; and as he hurried through the door she began to smooth out the tissue paper. Her eyes were so blinded that her hands had to find their way by their own instinct.

In the outer office Gillespie pulled from his ears the stethoscope with which he was listening to the heart of a man who stood before him, naked to the waist.

'You'll get them out there and be back tomorrow, Jimmy,' he directed.

'I'll be back as soon as possible,' said Kildare.

'As soon as possible?' roared Gillespie. 'I'm giving you a schedule. See that you run on time. Back here tomorrow, without fail, Medwick or no Medwick!'

He could not tell whether or no Kildare had

76

heard him, for the interne was already passing through the door.

'No fool like a young fool,' said the patient, sympathetically.

*   *   *

The office of young Dr Martin Whalen was up on the third floor; you walked to get to it. Kildare found not Whalen but a lad of fourteen who said: 'Doctor Whalen is out on a call. Just nearby. I'll tell him you're here. If you'll just sit down for a minute, sir. Here's some magazines. Be back in two minutes.'

Kildare sat down. He got up as the lad disappeared through the doorway and followed the clatter of feet down the stairs, down the freezing sidewalk outside, down a narrow alley, and to the back of a grocery store where a chunk of a young man was unloading boxes from a truck.

To him the boy was talking in great excitement and the other was stripping off an apron and nodding as he rolled down his sleeves, for the work had been hot even in this weather.

'Hello, Midge,' said Kildare.

'Ah—you?' said Whalen. 'I thought it was somebody worth while.'

'A rich guy with stomach trouble?' asked Kildare.

'Yes. And with three children, all married;

and three families of kids all with rickets; lots of dough and no brains.'

'You're going where there's two thousand kids that need you.'

'Siam or China, eh?'

'Do you care?'

'Not if it's medicine, and kids, and enough for bread and water and one beer on Saturday evening.' He grinned.

'Come on with me and pack your grip. We're going some place.'

'If I walk out on this job, I'm fired. And this is better than nothing. What are you offering?'

'A long shot.'

'All right, Jimmy. I was always a gambler.'

*   *   *

Dentist Sidney Garfield had the cat swathed in a bath towel to nullify those sharp claws, and her jaws propped open with a cork from a bottle.

'But you're not going to *cut* her!' screamed the little girl who watched with her sweating hands clasped together.

'Take him away! Don't let him touch poor Mike!' cried her brother.

'I've got to—'

'Don't!' screamed the children in chorus.

'There—you see all that stuff coming out? That ulcerated tooth was poisoning Mike.

78

Now he'll get well and fat. We swab on this stuff to make it heal quickly. Now we let poor Mike go, and you'll see how much happier he is already because...'

'Down to cat?' asked Kildare, as he leaned in the open doorway.

'Yeah. I'm Santa Claus,' said the dentist.

'How about setting up shop in the sticks?' asked Kildare.

'Sure,' said Garfield. 'All I want to see are teeth. I don't care who wears them.'

'Not much dough in it, Sid.'

'Anything is plus to my minus. You can't disappoint me, Jimmy?'

*　　　*　　　*

'If you come in,' roared the great voice in the sub-basement, 'bring enough cops with you to save your hide.'

Kildare pushed the door open and blinked at the dim light inside. The narrow cellar-room probably was served by a ventilator; but the air in it was like the air in a deep cave.

There was an iron cot with a single blanket dropped in a heap on it. Along the two walls were improvised shelves covered with test tubes and bottles that gave out foul aromas.

In the centre of the room stood huge Ben Connor, his face smudged with a seven days' beard as with soot. His hair fell forward in a great jag across his forehead so that he seemed all beast and no man at all.

'What is it, Ben; moonshine?' asked Kildare.

The big fellow took a lumbering step nearer to Kildare before recognition came to him.

'Hi, Jimmy,' he said. 'I thought you were that landlord again.'

'You've fixed up a regular garden for yourself,' said Kildare, sniffing.

'The bug I'm culturing is happy in a lot worse places than this,' said Ben Connor.

'Are you getting anywhere with it?'

'Sure. A couple more years, maybe, and I'll arrive with something.'

'Look, Ben, there's a little hick town that doesn't want young doctors, but the young doctors want it. Are you one of them?'

'You mean we have to break in?'

'Just about.'

Ben Connor lifted and spread his huge hands.

'I've been waiting a long time for a chance to use these,' he said.

*   *   *

'How do things go?' asked Kildare.

'Why, I'm keeping pretty busy. Too busy to move out of this dump, you see. An appendectomy and a fractured skull and a broken arm and a skin cancer, all yesterday.

'Things are waking up and I'm going to let my light shine; can't keep it under a bushel,

80

Jimmy,' said Darnell. 'Have a drink? No, you don't drink this time of day.'

'Yes, I'll have a drink,' said Kildare. 'It's Christmas, and all that.'

'Wait a minute,' said Darnell, rummaging through his kitchenette. 'Shucks—nothing but dead men. I forgot there were some of the boys in here last night.'

'Maybe I can find something,' said Kildare, and pulled open the second door of the pantry.

A chunk of old yellow cheese and the heel of a stale loaf were the only things in it.

'Haven't been eating in for a long time,' said Darnell.

'How long is it since you ate anywhere?' asked Kildare.

'Are you trying to kid yourself, or me?' asked Darnell, coldly.

'It's cold in here,' said Kildare, and turned on the gas switch at the grate. There was no answering hiss. He turned the switch back again.

'That thing's been out of order since yesterday,' said Darnell. 'But it doesn't bother me. Gas heat rots the oxygen in the air of a room, you know. There's altogether too much heat used, anyway.'

'That's a twenty-five cent meter,' said Kildare, 'isn't it?'

'I suppose it is,' agreed Darnell, carelessly. He shifted away from the eye of Kildare. A silence followed.

'I've got to run along, Jimmy,' said Darnell. 'Terribly sorry about the drink ... boys cleaned me out last night, as I was saying ... I have to get down to Maynard's hospital to look at a couple of patients and then ...'

He stood at the door, waiting for Kildare to go past him, but Kildare remained fixed in the centre of the room. They stared at one another for a moment.

After a moment Darnell closed the door, slowly.

'All right,' he said. 'You win.'

'Listen to me, Sammy,' said Kildare. 'There's a little town out there on the edge of Connecticut called Medwick ...'

* * *

There was a Christmas wreath on the door of Jack Davison's room. It was a single spray of fir, the kind you can buy for a quarter. Kildare looked at it for a moment, gloomily, before he knocked.

The door was opened by Davison himself. He paused for an instant, startled, then stepped out into the hall.

'Sorry I can't ask you in, Jimmy,' he said. 'But Joan's asleep.'

'We'd better wake her up,' said Kildare.

'I don't think so, old fellow,' answered Davison. 'I really don't. She's tired and all that. You know how she is, just now.'

'I know,' said Kildare, 'but don't act this way. I want to see Joan.'

'All right,' said Davison, making a slow surrender. 'But the fact is—'

'I understand,' said Kildare. 'Quit making excuses.'

When he went into the room, he saw Joan sitting up in the 'living-room' corner knitting. The only sign of Christmas hung outside on the door. There was not a token of it within the room.

Joan Davison started to get up, hastily, but Kildare prevented her.

'So nice of you to remember us, Jimmy,' she cried, 'but I'm afraid that it's going to be a gloomy spot in your day. You see, Jack and I both feel that all the Christmas to-do is rather silly and we made up our minds just to let the whole thing slide, and—'

'Why do you apologise to me, Joan?' he asked.

'It's no good,' explained Davison. 'He has the X-ray eye that Gillespie talks about. If we lie to him, he'll simply read our minds.

'Well, you know what the truth is, Jimmy. This is the only kind of a Christmas that I could afford to give her.'

After he had said that they were both easier; they were able now to be glad of Kildare's presence there. Joan smiled at him.

'I've come with a beggarly sort of a present for you both,' said Kildare. 'There's a town

83

without doctors called Medwick not so far away. The idea is for us to get together a group of doctors and try to take care of the whole place.

'The town's nearly broke so I can't try to bring in established practitioners. They have to be on the make, like you.

'There's a chance that the whole thing will crash through, too. We may not get the confidence of the Yankees in the village and then everything would be cooked. But I've got Midge Whalen signed up as pediatrist; Ben Connor as gynæcologist—'

'That big black devil is tops,' said Davison.

Kildare nodded and went on a little hurriedly.

'Sid Garfield will be the dentist, and Sammy Darnell will be general surgeon—'

'He has the greatest pair of hands I ever saw work,' said Davison. 'They can't beat down a crew like that. You mean that there'd be a place for me, Jimmy?'

'They have to have a laboratory man and an internist; you'd fill those two bills at a stroke,' declared Kildare.

'Do you hear, Joan?' cried Davison. 'It's our ship coming in! It's our chance!'

She was smiling, but there was doubt in her eyes above the smile.

'What would happen to Jack's job in the hospital?' she asked. 'That would have to go?'

'I'm afraid so,' said Kildare.

84

Her eyes were steadily on her husband; she did not look at Kildare as she went on questioning him.

'And nothing in Medwick is really sure?'

'Nothing is really sure.'

'Jack, can you afford to take the chance?'

'There's never a sure thing, when a doctor makes his start,' said Davison. 'Look at Jimmy, here. He thinks it's the right thing.'

'I think there could be a bare living and something more, perhaps—if it works out,' said Kildare.

'*If* it works out—you see?' said the girl.

'But it's got to work out. Jimmy's in it himself,' said Davison.

'Oh, that's different,' she agreed, turning back to Kildare. 'Are you really in it, Jimmy? You can't leave the hospital, can you?'

He looked into his thoughts for a moment. There was an abyss of doubt opening coldly before him as he thought of the last words of Gillespie and of all that might be entailed in a promise.

Then with a great lifting of the heart he overstepped the question and said calmly: 'I'm in the thing to stick; I'm in it until it begins to work, Joan.'

The change in her face then made him forget entirely the sudden, terrible doubt of a moment before.

'Are you, Jimmy? Are you, dear?' she insisted, brightening every instant. 'Then of

85

course it's all right for Jack. Of course—it's glorious—it makes this a *real* Christmas... I'm going to dance or something!'

*   *   *

When Kildare was down in the street again, he headed back toward the hospital rapidly; and as he leaned into the wind it seemed to him that he was pulling, on an invisible tow-line, six adult lives.

They were a present which Medwick might thank God for, or else they were a nuisance which Medwick would throw into the fire.

Five of them could endure the shock, no doubt; but for Joan Davison, he knew, failure might be a tragedy.

He went on down the street with his head lowered, and his uncertainty and his new fear were like a huge burden on him.

A great blasting of horns and ringing of bells turned a corner toward him. Half a dozen Christmas floats were rolling slowly through the streets. Windows were flying open and crowds gathering and shouting along the pavements.

On every float there was some sort of a stunt performing with plenty of girls bare enough for the Christmas beaches of Florida or California.

On the central float an enormous Santa Claus poured blessings upon the world with a megaphone.

Kildare was aware, suddenly, that there still was sunlight in the day, there still were unconcernedly happy people in the world— and it was Christmas!

He laughed a little. Hope unexpectedly had returned to him.

CHAPTER TEN

GOOD DOCTORS ARE BEGGARS

Back in the hospital, Kildare gave to Gillespie the list of his chosen men—those five young doctors willing to take a long shot on the town of Medwick.

'Why show the names to me?' demanded Gillespie. 'They're your men, not mine. Old men don't know young ones. We guess about you, but we never really know.

'You're like people in story-books. So go ahead with your gang. They'll take the glory, and you'll take the kicks in the face; and so, pretty soon, you'll be a little older.'

'We'll need medical supplies and a lot of them,' said Kildare.

'Go beg them from Walter Carew,' said Gillespie. 'That's something that a doctor has to be. He has to be a beggar. He has to beg to have his bill paid today; and tomorrow he has to beg rich blighters to help his charity patients. So learn how to get down and humble yourself without knee pads. Go beg from Carew!'

Kildare stared at him.

'You think I'm unfair?' roared Gillespie suddenly. 'What the devil will you do when you have to handle this whole office unless you know how to work Carew—or somebody a damned sight harder?'

Kildare went up to see Carew. He was admitted at once.

'Merry Christmas,' said Carew. 'Now run along, Kildare. I'm busy. Come back another day.'

'Another day will be too late,' said Kildare.

'For what?' asked Carew.

'For an ambulance load of drugs and medicines and all sorts of supplies that are needed in Medwick.'

'An ambulance load? What's Medwick to me or me to Medwick? Am I the state dispensary? What made you think the hospital would give out like this?'

'I thought that it was Christmas,' said Kildare.

'Did you? Did Gillespie send you here on a fool's errand of this sort?'

'You seemed the only person to turn to,' said Kildare.

'Did Gillespie send you here?'

'You understand, Doctor Carew, that I wouldn't come to you except in a great emergency.'

'You're covering up Gillespie, are you?' demanded Carew. He stopped glowering and leaned suddenly back in his chair. 'I wonder who'd cover up old Carew if *he* did something foolish? Who'd take the rap for *me*?...

'Well, make out your list and perhaps I'll look it over one of these days.'

'I have the list here, sir.'

'You have the list there, have you? Let me see it. Good Lord, Kildare, there's a thousand dollars' worth of stuff on this list. There's more than that. It's entirely irregular. I'd be held to account. I can't do it. Sorry, but I can't do it.'

'No, sir,' said Kildare.

'It can't be expected of me.'

'No, sir,' said Kildare.

'I can't be expected to play Santa Claus all over the place, can I?'

'No, sir,' said Kildare.

'Then why don't you get out and leave me in peace?'

'Because I hope you'll talk yourself into the Christmas spirit, sir.'

'You have an infernal, assured brazen way about you,' said Carew. 'You seem to think that you're always right. Part of the time I suppose you are. Well, here's my okay on the thing. Take it away.'

He returned the list to Kildare with his

signature added to it.

'This means a lot to a great many people,' said Kildare. 'Thank you, sir.'

'Let other people do the thanking—and let them thank your infernal stubbornness ... How is Gillespie?'

'Better than he was last week.'

'He bears up,' murmured Carew. 'God bless him, the man's body may be eaten away, but his spirit endures. There's no consuming that.'

'When you see your son, give him my regards, sir.'

'What do you think of that lad?'

'I think he's a fine fellow. He's different from the rest of us,' said Kildare, looking hard at Carew, 'but I hope he'll find a lot of happiness.'

'He'll find it,' stated Carew. 'I've made a good many mistakes about that boy, but I'm on the right line with him, at last.'

'I'm glad of that, sir,' said Kildare, immensely relieved.

'Sometimes we waste a great deal of time before we know our own; but I know William now, and he'll be on a good footing with me and with life from now on.'

Kildare went from the office with his head high, and there was a song that worked mutely in his throat.

Late that night he had the ambulance-load of materials deposited in the Lancey house. Old Mrs Lancey, helpless with rheumatism in her bedroom, freely donated the rest of her old house, together with the long dairy-shed behind it, to the uses of the doctors.

The whole thing split up into domains. There was even an end room of the dairy-shed in which Jack Davison was setting up the first elements of a small laboratory. All night they worked putting their affairs in order.

In the early morning, Geoffrey Winslow visited the house and walked through all the arrangements. Old Stephen Kildare and his son walked anxiously beside the chief power and mind of Medwick.

There were not many questions. Winslow seemed to prefer to do his own looking and draw his own deductions in silence. He was introduced to all of the young doctors and gave them all a brief, hard grip of the hand, and a grave scanning.

Afterward he said to Stephen Kildare: 'I like to see a small seed planted and then watch it grow. But here there's a whole tree transplanted, from the taproot to the top bough ... I hope Medwick is the right sort of soil to nurture it.'

'You've broken the ground for us,' said James Kildare. 'You've put yourself behind us and that ought to be enough if these doctors can work the way I know they want to work.'

'I hope for the best,' said Winslow, his grim face never relaxing. 'I can't help noticing that your child specialist looks like a prizefighter and your obstetrician looks like a longshoreman and your general surgeon acts like a tap dancer or a gigolo, but still I hope for the best. I know you've picked out the right people as nearly as you can, Dr Kildare.'

Stephen Kildare said: 'The actual selections were made by my son, Mr Winslow.'

Winslow was stopped and hard hit by this announcement.

'This young man?' he exclaimed. 'Did *he* do the choosing?'

'You know, Mr Winslow,' said the old doctor, 'that my time is spent chiefly in the country. I don't have an opportunity to rub elbows with the youngsters who are coming up in medicine. So of course I left the choosing to my son. He has an instinct for the right man.'

Winslow surveyed young Kildare with his customary air of cold reservation.

'There's a financial aspect to this,' he said, leaving his mind on the last subject unspoken. 'I've designed a way in which Medwick, no matter how poor the people are, can afford to secure proper medical services from such a group as these young doctors form.

'There are three thousand people in the town. At ten cents per week per head, that would give us fifteen thousand dollars a year. And that ought to pay small salaries to the five doctors as well as pay for medicines.

'Hospitalisation would be another thing to think about. We could perhaps pay two thousand a year to each of the doctors and leave the margin for medical supplies.'

Stephen Kildare said, reflectively:

'After twenty-three or four years of special education, a man must content himself with an income of two thousand a year? Thirty or forty dollars a week, when ordinary labour . . .'

He broke off.

Jimmy Kildare said: 'None of them expects to get rich. They want a chance to make a beginning.'

Winslow remained coldly formal. He said: 'It will be necessary to hold a town meeting and discuss this business in a few days. By that time, Medwick will have had the chance to see the new doctors at work.

'If the town is favourably impressed, I've no doubt that the meeting will vote to assess each head in the town at the rate I've suggested. The matter is now in the hands of your associates, Dr Kildare. They will have to prove or disprove themselves in the interim.'

With this, he left the Kildares abruptly and walked out of the house.

'He's a hard man, but he's just,' said Stephen Kildare.

'Something has worn him out,' said Jimmy.

'His cares and worries about the town,' suggested Stephen Kildare.

'It's more than that,' answered Jimmy, and shook his head. 'Will you go home, now, and go to bed?'

'Wouldn't it be better for me to stay here

until your friends have made their start?'

'No. They have to make or break themselves. You can't hold people like them on leading strings.'

'Then I'm going home,' said the father, 'to sleep, and sleep, and sleep!'

Kildare went up to Joan Davison and found her still tidying up her room. At this moment she was putting Davison's diplomas on the wall.

Against the window the rain struck heavily aslant and darkened the room to the shade and almost to the texture of a charcoal drawing.

Joan bloomed in the dimness. She hardly could speak without laughter.

'It's like the beginning of everything. It's like the first day of life,' she said. 'This is where Jack starts to show the world what he is!'

'It's not all settled,' Kildare warned her, and he kept the grim face of Winslow always in mind. 'We have to go along slowly but in the end the thing will go through. These are pretty stubborn people, Joan.'

'Don't they want to be helped?' she asked.

'They want to be helped—in the ways they're accustomed to. I've tried to warn the boys to go slowly. But I'm only an interne, Joan, and they're all my superior officers. I have to talk small.'

'Superior officers? Superior to *you*, Jimmy?' She laughed at him.

He said soberly: 'If things should begin to go

94

badly, in your estimation, I want you to telephone to me. Nobody else will. Promise me that you'll do it?'

'Of course I will. But where's the danger?'

'They may try to give Medwick many good things in a rush instead of one by one. But if a pinch comes, perhaps I can be of help.'

'Of course they'll shout for you if there's trouble!'

'Doctors never shout for internes. I'll depend on you to let me know, Joan.'

'I'll keep a whole diary for you,' she said.

'You keep yourself,' said Kildare.

CHAPTER ELEVEN

A TOWN BEWITCHED

Two days later Mrs Anthony Cabot and Mrs Peter Devlin came through the Medwick rain to call on Geoffrey Winslow. He received them not in a living-room but in a parlour; for Winslow was proud of the virtues of his ancestors and approved all their ways of living, even down to their 'Sunday' room.

'It's my well, Mr Winslow!' said Mrs Peter Devlin, fat and busy. 'You know the water of that well?'

'Everyone knows it,' said Winslow. 'Has something fallen in?'

'You remember the day you were talking with Peter ten years ago about money for the new barn and it was hot and you wanted a glass of water and you said it was the finest water you'd ever tasted?'

'Everyone knows it's the finest water in the town,' said Winslow. 'Sit down, please.'

Mrs Cabot sat down but Mrs Peter Devlin was bursting with indignation.

'*You* may know, Mr Winslow, but what you know,' she said, 'isn't good enough for *some* people, with their crazy, new-fangled ideas! It's not good enough for these new, baby-faced boys who call themselves doctors!'

'I've been hearing about them,' said Winslow. 'What's up now?'

'You wouldn't believe it,' said she. 'It's just too much to be believed, but one of them ordered me to seal that well. He didn't ask. He ordered!'

'You didn't make them constables, Mr Winslow, I hope?' asked Mrs Anthony Cabot.

'I made them nothing,' he answered with firmness. 'Who was this one and what were his reasons?'

'This is the one called Whalen.'

'The fellow who looks like a prizefighter?'

'That's the man! How could he be a doctor—how could he, above all, be a *child* specialist? Oh, Mr Winslow, he showed me some stuff in little glass tubes and talked about germs and said that my Susie Anne and all the Wheeler

96

children were sick from drinking the water of that well; and he said that he directed me to seal that well immediately.

'And, Mr Winslow, if I close that well I'll have to pipe in town water and we haven't any money and Peter's been out of work so long.'

'Have you closed the well?' asked the calm voice of Winslow.

'No, sir. I haven't closed it yet.'

'Then I wouldn't,' said Winslow.

'Thank you, Mr Winslow. I just knew what you would say!'

'And what trouble have you been having, Mrs Cabot?'

'It turns out my hams and bacons are no good,' said Mrs Cabot, crisply.

'We have one of your sides of bacon in the house right now,' said Winslow. 'I never tasted better bacon.'

'No matter what you and the others think,' said Mrs Cabot. 'The bacon has to be hauled out and burned. Even burning wouldn't be safe enough. Young Davison, who called himself a doctor, says that it's no good. It's got to go.'

'Why?' asked Winslow.

'Because there's something in it. It's nothing you can see. It's nothing you can smell. It's nothing you can taste. But it's dangerous.'

'Ah? Dangerous?' murmured Winslow.

'He says so,' declared Mrs Cabot, disdainfully. 'He says that probably Abe Jenkins' family and Cousin Harry Wharton's boys are sick from my bacon, and heaven knows how many else!'

'And why not I and my wife and everyone else who has eaten the bacon?' asked Winslow.

'I can't tell. Something about your people frying bacon crisper, or some nonsense such as that. Mr Winslow, he laid a death at my door! He dared to say that poor, sweet Annie McIvor must have died last year from eating meat from my smoke-house.'

'I think that smoke-house,' said Winslow, calmly, 'has been working for two hundred years or more. Yes, more. It was built ten years after the house. That was in 1723. And in all that time I don't think anyone has pointed a wrong finger at the Cabots. I know Medwick, Mrs Cabot, and I don't think anyone has pointed a wrong finger at the Cabots!'

Tears of pleasure stood up in the eyes of Mrs Cabot. She could not speak until she had risen to go.

'So I won't bury it!' she exploded, then.

'I never like to see good food wasted,' said Winslow. 'What do these young doctors think they're about?'

'Why,' said Mrs Cabot, 'I think they believe that our town is hexed!'

'Medwick? Bewitched? Our Medwick?'

Winslow, who almost never laughed, managed to smile.

'What's to be done about them?' demanded Mrs Anthony Cabot.

'Why, there's a town meeting in a few days,' said Winslow, 'and then I should not be surprised if something were done about the doctors that would be more than sufficient—yes, very much more than sufficient!'

In the meantime, Mrs Winslow in her upstairs sitting-room, with the round rag rug before the little hearth and the window curtains puffed and starched until they were as stiff as stone, was saying to her niece:

'I wouldn't talk to him about it just now, Barbara.'

'But I've always talked to Uncle Geoffrey about everything!' said Barbara. 'And it's only such a tiny little bit of a thing to ask, after all. He doesn't use the Pinewood at all, does he?'

'No, he hasn't used it for two or three years. But he's not in a giving mood or even in a lending mood, Barbara darling,' said Mrs Winslow.

'Uncle Geoffrey,' queried the girl. 'Why, he's given and loaned all his life!'

'It's the dying of Medwick that's changed him,' whispered Mrs Winslow.

'Oh, but Medwick's not dying, is it?'

'Slowly dying, and sometimes I almost think that your Uncle Geoffrey is dying with it.'

'Aunt Marian!'

'God forgive me if I'm drumming up trouble and crossing bridges before I come to them,' said Mrs Winslow, 'but every day, it seems to me, there's less life in his eye, and there's less of a ring in his voice, and his step is slower.'

'Has he lost so much money?' asked Barbara, aghast.

'It's not the money that matters to him,' said his wife. 'But Medwick is his whole blood and bone. It gave him his fortune and he loves it. He knows all the people in it. He's loaned and fended and helped with advice, but now it seems to me that he's beginning to love the people less than the town.

'I think there's a little hardness and suspicion creeping into him, like old age, like bitter old age that's come on him before his time!'

'There he is now,' said Barbara. 'He's through with those women. I'm going down and ask him, this minute.'

'Oh, Barbara. I wouldn't if I were you.'

'Why not? Murray's as proud as steel. He wouldn't have let me come to ask for the Pinewood cottage if he'd thought that it was begging.'

'It's not begging, darling, but … Barbara, please don't go!'

'Aunt Marian, I know Uncle Geoffrey. He's never said no to me in his life.'

She hurried out of the room and ran down the stairs. Mrs Winslow, breathlessly listening, clasped her hands together and bowed her head a little over them. Even in this moment of dread, she could not help noticing and adoring the lightness with which the girl's footfall went down the stairs.

Then she heard Barbara singing out: 'Uncle Geoffrey, Murray and I wondered—if you're not using it—if we could have the Pinewood cottage for a couple of months?'

There was a pause, Mrs Winslow closed her eyes and winced from the blow. Then the hard, dry voice of her husband was saying: 'Go back to Murray Allister and tell him that in my time I've grown used to men *paying* for the roofs over their heads.'

There was a faint cry from Barbara. The heavy step of Winslow went on toward the rear of the house; and after a moment another footfall, pausing, timid, began to come back up the stairs.

Mrs Winslow went suddenly out to the head of the steps and waited for the girl, but Barbara came up to her and passed as if she were not there. In the little sitting-room again she stood in front of the window as if she were looking out at a new world, although, in fact, the rain had made the glass as opaque as dark, deep water.

CHAPTER TWELVE

YOU WILL DIE...

The voice of Joan Davison came over the telephone to Kildare thin and small, like that of a lost child: 'Is it wrong to tell you that I'm afraid things are very bad here, Jimmy? No one will talk to me. They're afraid that I'll find out something.

'But, Jimmy, no more patients are coming to the house. Hardly a one, and I know that Jack and the rest of them all are frightened... It's silly for me to bother you, Jimmy, only you told me to let you know.'

'Has my father come back to Medwick?' asked Kildare.

'Yes, I saw him yesterday.'

'Then it's time for me to get out there,' said Kildare. 'I'll come today.'

'... Medwick? You'll go back to Medwick? For what? And who'll let you go?' demanded Gillespie.

'They're having trouble with the town,' said Kildare. 'I thought that I might be useful to them in some way.'

'If five real doctors can't wangle the thing, how can an interne succeed?'

'I don't know, sir. It's just a matter of seeing what I could do.'

'Or maybe,' said Gillespie, 'you've turned into a diplomat. Kind of an international diplomat. Going to stop being a doctor, perhaps, and cure people with tact. Is that it? Better send young Doctor Kildare over to St James's, so's he can wear short pants and talk to the king, eh? ... What in tophet would you be doing over there in Medwick?'

'I don't know,' repeated Kildare, 'but sometimes there's a way of working things—if you put your muscle into it. I'd like to go out there again, sir, if you don't mind.'

'Have you got a plan of campaign?'

'No, sir.'

'What do you intend doing?'

'I intend to talk to Mr Winslow.'

'Why Winslow?'

'Because if there's trouble, I imagine he's making it.'

'What makes you say that?'

'I don't know, sir. I've an instinct that he might make trouble.'

'All right, Kildare. I know you. You want to get close and fire when you see the whites of their eyes.'

'May I go, sir?'

'That's not the question. The question is when you'll return.'

'It looks like a quick fight, and then a finish, one way or the other.'

'Will you quit when you're beaten?'

'Beaten? I suppose so, sir.'

'We'll have to see about that. Well, go along, go along! You're no good to me here when your heart's in another place!'

Before Kildare reached Medwick, matters had progressed very far. Midge Whalen, looking more like a chunk of prizefighter than ever, stood in the centre of the parlour of the Lancey cottage and stated the condition exactly.

Connor, Darnell, and Sid Garfield sat deeply slouched in their chairs, looking at the pattern of the rug. Davison was upstairs with his wife.

'Joan is hard hit,' said Whalen. 'She tied her whole hope of the future to this business and now she's sunk. We're all hit pretty hard, but she's sunk without a trace, now that this Medwick business is a dead loss.'

'You mean there's not a ghost of hope?' asked Kildare.

'How can there be,' demanded Whalen, 'when the head man is set dead against us?'

'Winslow? I'll try to talk to him,' said Kildare.

'You talked us into this mess, but you'll never be able to talk us out again,' snarled Connor.

Whalen said, 'Quit that, Ben!'

'All right. I'm sorry,' said Connor. 'That was just some of the black Irish coming out of me. Forget it, Jimmy, will you?'

Kildare waved a hand and shrugged his

shoulders. He went upstairs to the Davisons. They were full of a sort of courteously smiling despair. They did not blame Kildare. They did not have to. Their silence was more than enough.

'What's happened?' asked Kildare. 'I don't make much sense out of it, except that Winslow seems to be set against you.'

'He's sent out word that we're a lot of young fools,' said Davison. 'He has the people in the town afraid to come to us because they'll be laughed at.'

'What are his reasons?' asked Kildare.

'I don't know. All I know is that the townspeople talk behind our backs when we go down the street. We can stand that, all right; we could stand it if even a few of them would start coming to us for treatment.

'But the main thing is that there's the town meeting tomorrow to decide whether or not they should levy a poll tax in order to pay us; the way you said they would. And Winslow will sink us at the meeting.'

Kildare stood by the window and tapped his fingertips against the cold glass. He was silent for a long moment.

'You see?' he heard the almost inaudible voice of Davison say behind him.

'He's not finished. He'll think out something to do,' answered the whisper of Joan.

Kildare turned and looked at the girl. She made herself smile at him. She was white and

105

very frightened; the tell-tale bruises of insomnia were around her eyes; but she attached some sort of a blind hope to Kildare.

'That's right, Joan,' he said. 'I'm going to find something to do. I'm going to try the first step now.'

She began to weep. She fought so hard against giving way that the sobbing was deep and half strangled like that of a man unused to breaking down.

Kildare left the Lancey house and went straight to the bank of Geoffrey Winslow. All that the sign announced was *Real Estate*; but there was a back room with a few old mahogany chairs and a roll-topped desk in it that served as the only bank the town of Medwick knew.

Kildare had to wait outside the door of clouded glass and he could not help hearing the raised tones of Winslow, saying: 'You're not beaten in fact, Parker. You're only beaten in fancy, the way the whole town is beaten. You sit down and fold your hands...'

'No, sir,' said a tremulous voice. 'I've been all around. I've asked for work everywhere.'

'There's no use asking for work,' said Winslow. 'There's no use asking for it, in a time like this. This is the time to make work. That's why God gave you a brain. To create—to make something where there was nothing before.

'Go out and do that and don't come in here whining that you can't pay your interest. I'm not your grandfather. I've no paternal interest in you.

'The trouble is that I've treated the whole lot of you as though you were children, but now I'm going to make you be men. You have to stand on your own feet. You understand?'

'Yes, sir,' said Parker.

'You can have till Monday to find that money, Parker,' said Winslow. 'That's all.'

Chairs pushed back. Parker came out from the door with Winslow standing behind him. Parker's desperate face made Kildare think of a battle picture: men charging in a lost cause and knowing that they are about to fall.

Winslow said: 'Ah, it's young Doctor Kildare. What can I do for you, young man?'

Parker, moving on, gradually slowed and then turned to listen. Behind the desks in the outer room, Winslow's two assistants were staring at Kildare and smiling a little. They seemed to anticipate what was to come.

'I'm afraid that you don't approve of the new doctors,' said Kildare.

'Perhaps not, entirely,' said Winslow. 'You see, I'm an old-fashioned man, young Doctor Kildare, but I'm not so old that I believe in witchcraft.'

Kildare waited. He could feel that doom was about to descend upon this medical experiment in Medwick, but there was something else that kept him staring at the banker: there was something in Winslow's face and something about the drag of his voice, no matter how loud it might be, that intrigued the diagnostician's instinct of Kildare.

He was reading in the man far more than he was hearing from him.

Winslow enlarged a little on his theme: 'In the days of witchcraft the credulity of people was more elastic; but though I know that young men *must* get our attention, even if they have to scream at the top of their voices, I'm not quite prepared for it when they say that because several families become ill down by the river, John Heney's cow should be shot at the top of the hill!'

There was stifled laughter from the people in the background.

Kildare said: 'But if Heney has been delivering milk and there is a disease appearing among his—'

'My lad,' said Winslow, 'I'm not a complete fool. I realize that there are such things as germs. Even in Medwick we read the newspapers—now and then. It isn't the cow on the hill alone.

'Take the case of Mrs Finney's barn. Because a good many people have colds in the head in the western part of the town, it appears that your very young friends want to burn down Mrs Finney's barn! She objects, I object; and I'm afraid that the barn shall not be burned.'

'Mr Winslow,' said Kildare, 'if the hay is a

source of hay-fever and the barn itself is—'

'Is covered with witchcraft?' sneered Winslow. 'But there are other things. Peter Devlin's well—the best water in town!—is to be stopped; the Cabots' fine sides of bacon are to be buried like a plague; and finally—God forgive us!—all milk is to be taken away from the Turner baby. He's to have what, instead? Why, young Doctor Kildare, he's to have bean-soup!'

There was a sudden roar of laughter from the others though Winslow seemed not even tempted to smile.

Kildare said: 'In certain cases soya beans must be used when...'

'Young man,' said Winslow, 'there is always an explanation for everything, if one cares to look far enough for it. But Medwick has had enough of the medical gymnastics of your friends. We don't want them here, Doctor Kildare. In fact, we don't intend to have them.'

'I see how it is,' said Kildare.

'What do you see?' asked Winslow.

'You've set the town solidly against us,' said Kildare. 'Through the whole of Medwick, perhaps one person in five needs medical attention. You have scores of chronic cases that either are incurable, now, or soon will be; but because sound doctors are telling you how to prevent disease at the same time that they attempt to cure it, you're going to throw them out of the place.'

109

'No throwing, my friend,' said Winslow. 'We wouldn't waste that much effort on them.'

'However, you won't oppose the doctors very long.'

'Won't I? We have had witchcraft, and now we're to have prophecy, it seems?'

'Mr Winslow, you've been finding it, recently, a little more of an effort to walk about; a chair is pretty welcome to you?'

'Why should a man stand when he can sit?' asked Winslow.

'There is a great deal of soreness in your mouth and around your tongue, isn't there?'

'Dr Kildare, I have work to do. It isn't my practice, after all, to waste my time in mere gossip. I'll say good-bye to you.'

'Wait a moment,' said Kildare. 'I wanted to tell you why you've lost your good nature, why there's that soreness in your mouth, why it's harder for you to get about, just the past few days—and why you won't interfere with the doctors very much longer.'

'Ah, can you tell me that?' asked Winslow. 'What is the answer, then?'

'You are about to die,' said Kildare.

Winslow, narrowing his eyes, stared fixedly at Kildare. There was no more laughter in the room.

'If it seems like witchcraft to you,' said Kildare, 'I'm sorry. But your death may help to restore the reputation of the doctors. It may give Medwick a chance to fight intelligently for

110

its health.

'I hate to choose a date so soon, but I'm afraid that Mr Parker won't have to pay you that money on Monday. You won't be alive to receive it.'

CHAPTER THIRTEEN

GREETING FROM MARY

'Gone?' repeated Mary Lamont. 'Has Jimmy really gone, Doctor Gillespie?' Her voice was incredulous and a little hurt.

'This time he didn't say good-bye to you, eh? Yes, he's really gone. So far as I know, he's got his bulldog grip on another of his lost causes; and every time he locks his jaws that way, it may be the end of him. It may mean that he'll be dragged down to the bottom of the sea without letting go.'

She went back into Kildare's office and stood at his desk with her fingers idling through a stack of reports, and unsorted cards which would have to go into the indices.

There was no end to this indexing, since the whole world of medicine, to young Kildare, was qualified in every item by the comments of the great Gillespie.

She grew infinitely weary of the name of Gillespie; at times; it salted the conversation of

Kildare as verses from the Koran haunt the lips of the true believer.

She was unaware, now, of what her hands were doing. It was a small thing that had happened to her but it had shocked her into a great, new consciousness.

The ticking of a clock is a trifling annoyance as a rule, but now and again it makes us aware that time is carrying us away to the sea of darkness, and then we feel the old futility and the sudden sense of doom.

So with Mary Lamont this unannounced departure of Kildare was the light stroke that set a great bell ringing in her. She had been shaping her whole life and soul to the thought of Kildare; but what did she mean to him, after all? Love is of a thousand varieties, from the divine passion to the dull acceptance of stalled oxen.

Her unthinking hands now had turned over the desk papers to the very bottom of the pile; and there she saw again the note addressed to Kildare and marked 'Personal.' She remembered it now, with a shock.

In spite of the fact that he had passed it over casually with the remark that he was only an interne, not a person, she should have brought it to his attention again. Or, since he refused to read it, she should have opened it herself.

There are a thousand things which a patient may well feel should come under the eyes of the doctor alone; but a trained nurse also must be an impersonal creature.

Before she had finished this thought the envelope was opened and her eyes were reading the words of the note which had been written by Marguerite Paston and William Carew.

She glanced through it once and found it merely a note of adieu.

She read through it carefully a second time. It seemed to her startled mind that this was like an answer to the question which had been flung at her the moment before. What did she mean to Kildare?

Not what these two young lovers meant to one another, at least. For somehow, though nothing was stated definitely, the idea crept out from among the words that here were two who were ready to die, calmly, because the world would not accept them together.

Once more she studied the note and the idea seemed more vague than her surmise; but Jimmy Kildare would know the truth. He would catch up the implications instantly.

Perhaps it was already too late. Perhaps they already were dead; perhaps this rain which thrummed against the windows was beating against their faces.

She got leave of absence from Molly Cavendish and took the train for Dartford; from there she could get transportation to Medwick in a bus, in a taxi if there were no direct bus line.

Some three hours later she was in the house

113

of Stephen Kildare in Dartford. She had not been able to avoid the temptation to look in at the place where Jimmy had first found soil to grow in.

The old framed photographs, the rugs, the Victorian furniture, the very nature of the waxed floorboards would have meant vital things to her, even on the morning of this day.

Those grim faces along the wall would have seemed, this morning, the ancestors of her children-to-be; but now she was partially withdrawn from a state of mind and being that seemed to her like a dream.

This old woman with the loose folds of flesh in her face was nothing to her and never could be anything to her children, probably.

She felt that sense of time which is like a physical uncleanness. The faint odours of generations of cookery breathed out of these rooms and her spirit shrank from the entire scene.

Out of the mud of Dartford Kildare had grown, and something muddy and uninspired still remained in his nature. Let her rather have some shining youth, with a few centuries of high breeding and culture behind him...

She was being introduced to another girl of her own age, a Beatrice Raymond, who had come in bringing a fishing rod in a case. She had thrown a coat over her head and shoulders to protect her from the rain while she was running from the adjoining house.

It had just come to her, she said, that Jimmy had left the fishing rod in the old blacksmith's shop behind the barn.

'How in the world did you ever think about it, dear, after all this time?' asked Mrs Kildare.

'I was just wondering what would make Jimmy forget a fishing rod, you know. Then I remembered the day. We were coming in from the creek; and he saw Liz Atkins' dog limping across the field. He dropped the rod in the old shop and went after the dog to see what was wrong ... But there it is!'

She gave over the case to Mrs Kildare and left, only pausing at the door to say: 'How is the doctor?'

'He's working back at Medwick again,' said Mrs Kildare, 'but Jimmy's out there, too; so I suppose it'll be all right.'

'If Jimmy's there, everything will come out,' said Beatrice Raymond, and disappeared.

'She's really lovely, isn't she?' said Mary Lamont.

'Oh, it isn't her looks that count,' said Mrs Kildare. 'They're just the outside wrapping, but I know everything that's in that parcel and it's all good. I've known it for years, and it's every bit good. Even Jimmy used to think so, and maybe he'll think so again, but you know how he is; girls don't mean a great deal to him just now.'

'I suppose not,' said Mary Lamont.

'Working with him as much as you do, you

115

must have seen that girls don't excite him often; and when they do come along into his attention, it's only for a moment, and only a surface ripple at that.'

'I think that's true,' said Mary Lamont soberly.

'But just now he's working to make himself all that God meant him to be; and later on he'll open his eyes to other things. I hope it will be Beatrice, because a doctor's wife should be a patient woman, you know.'

'Of course,' said the girl, and to herself she was thinking: Patience, calm, gentleness, endurance, and hands far busier than the brain—that's what it takes to be a doctor's wife. And all the sheen and beauty of bright, active moments, excitement and hope, are lost to her.

There *are* such things. She carried in her purse a letter written by two people who perhaps felt that it was better to die rather than to permit that high and lonely expectation to be tarnished by the world.

There was another point of deadly importance: Jimmy had not found the time, he had not thought it worth while, perhaps, to tell his mother about her.

She said as she stood up to leave: 'I think Jimmy *will* come back to her, some day. I think I hope he does.'

'That's sweet of you,' said the mother. 'They'd make a pair who would work along

116

quietly to get the good things; just quiet and work, that's what does it.'

'Just quiet and work,' the girl kept saying to herself as the bus carried her toward Medwick. 'Quiet—work—then stooping shoulders—and all for a man who doesn't care? Not a great care, at least—not a care great enough to keep a Mary Lamont in his mind.'

She found the way to the Lancey cottage. No one answered her ring. Perhaps the uproar of the rain was too great for it to be heard.

She found the door unlatched and walked in. Muddy footprints tracked up and down the hall, some drying in a thin streaking of grey, most often still wet.

As she closed the door, she shut away so much of the violence of the storm that she could hear voices, clearly in the next room. She recognised the voice of Jack Davison saying: 'But what's the use hanging on until we're beaten to a pulp? We've lost already. Kildare, we're cooked. You always think that a thing can be bulldogged through, but we're cooked.'

'Absolutely,' said another. 'Particularly since you had your scene with Winslow. Good Lord, Jimmy, how could you have been wild enough to set a date line? How could you have been crazy enough to tell the man that he'd be dead before Monday?'

'You've heard that, have you?' asked the voice of Kildare, and she recognised in its extreme quiet the absolute grimness of his

117

fighting mood.

'Of course I've heard it,' said another. 'The whole town is talking about it and laughing at you. Winslow is laughing, too.'

'No,' said Kildare. 'Winslow isn't laughing. Whatever is happening, Winslow isn't laughing, I'd say.'

'The fact is,' said another, 'you've done us in, Kildare! I think we would have had a fighting chance, but you've done us in. When you talked to Winslow and lost your temper, you cut the last ground from under our feet!'

'I didn't lose my temper. I told him the truth,' said Kildare.

'Come, come, Kildare,' broke in a highly irritated voice. 'You've been working with Gillespie; you've done yourself pretty proud a number of times; but don't let it go to your head; don't try to make yourself into a prophet. I've *seen* Winslow, and I've seen him at close range. I didn't see anything wrong with him except his Yankee meanness sticking out at every pore.'

'You can't talk like that to Jimmy,' said Davison, suddenly.

'What'll keep me from it?'

'I'll keep you!' said Davison.

'Back up!' said Kildare. 'Both of you, back up.'

'I'm going to knock his head off,' said Davison.

'I'll take care of my own dignity,' said

Kildare. 'I don't need help...'

The voices went on, sometimes shouting. Mary Lamont sat down in the hall and wrote in a fine hand on one of her cards:

Jimmy, dear, here is a letter that you must read. I hope it doesn't mean what I guess. Another thing I guess is that we don't mean to one another what these two mean. In fact, I wonder if there's anything important—really important—between us.

I've got a vacation coming to me and I'm taking it now. I need to do a lot of thinking.
MARY

P.S.—Don't for heaven's sake hang on in Medwick trying to do the impossible. Do for *once* believe what other people tell you instead of following your own stubborn instinct. Some day that same instinct may ruin your life. Dear Jimmy, be careful!

She had an impulse as soon as the note was written, to crumple it in her hand and throw it away; but after a moment she slid the note into the envelope and posted itself right on the ledge of the hall telephone where it could not fail to be seen.

After that, she left the house. The rain beat down on her with a thousand small, angry hands. She stopped, took a deep breath, and went resolutely on.

CHAPTER FOURTEEN

THE LONGEST NIGHT

Doctor Carew, as usual, was dropping one telephone and picking up another, snapping out his answers sharply. He was surprised by a voice as dry and brisk as his own, which said to him over the line:

'This is Kildare speaking. I'd like to know where your son is.'

'Back in the university, of course. What do you mean by breaking in on me with—'

'Because he's not at the university.'

Carew lost half his anger. It was replaced by astonishment.

'What makes you think that he's not?' he demanded.

'Ring the college, if you want to make sure. He hasn't been back since he talked with you the other day.'

'That's impossible,' said Carew.

'Nothing's impossible,' said Kildare. 'Not to a young man with any spirit when he's whipped up into a corner. I'd like to know what you said to him.'

'Who gives you the right to know what I say to my own son?' shouted Carew.

'The right to keep him from dying,' said Kildare.

120

'Dying? My God!' whispered Carew.

'Why not?' asked Kildare. 'You saw the girl. She's worth dying for, isn't she?'

'A baby—a baby hardly out of the cradle. Kildare, what are you saying?'

'I'm saying: Get on their trail, for God's sake. Ring the university first to make sure that he's not there. Then start on the trail; go to the girl's address; find out where they've been seen. They'll go together.'

'Kildare, are you talking about—about self-destruction? Are you telling me ... Kildare, how long will it take you to get here?'

'I can't leave Medwick till tomorrow. Perhaps I can't leave it then,' said Kildare. 'You've got to work alone, till then.

'But listen to me; unless you save them, you've thrown away something worth more than the whole hospital and all the people in it. Ring the university and get after them.'

Afterward, Kildare sat in the dimness of the hallway and read again the note which Mary Lamont had left for him: ... *We don't mean to one another what these two mean. In fact, I wonder if there's anything important ... between us.*

After a while he found his hands cold and rubbed them together but the chill would not leave him. It had penetrated his whole body as deep as the heart.

He went up to the room of the Davisons. Jack was packing; Joan lay on the bed with her

121

face to the wall.

'Take those things out and put them back in the bureau,' said Kildare.

Davison stared at him, fighting mad for an instant.

Then he changed and said, quietly: 'All right, Jimmy.'

'Are the others getting out?' asked Kildare.

'They're packing and all that. But I don't think they'll get out till you give the word. They're a little ashamed of the way they talked to you.'

'That doesn't matter,' said Kildare. He looked at Joan. The rain kept rattling steadily on the roof. There was a streak of fresh wetness down the wall beside the bed where the rain had found a leak in the roof.

He went over to the girl and sat down beside her. She put a hand back toward him without turning her head.

'Jimmy?'

'Yes,' he said.

'What are we going to do, Jimmy? We've *no* place to go to now.'

'There's still a hope right here in Medwick,' he said. She sat up breathless.

'There's still a sort of chance, and I'm going to take it now,' he said.

'You hear, Jack?' cried the girl. 'I *told* you that Jimmy Kildare couldn't be beaten as quickly as this!'

Davison followed him out into the hall. He

122

whispered: 'You shouldn't have said that, Jimmy.'

'Perhaps I shouldn't,' admitted Kildare.

'I know you're the sort to put your whole life on the turn of the card; but it'll break Joan to pieces, now, when you fail.'

'Perhaps it will,' said Kildare, and went down the stairs without another word.

He spent some time back in Davison's laboratory, then took his medical kit and walked through the rain to the house of Geoffrey Winslow.

At his ring the door was opened by Mrs Winslow. She, tall and pale as a stone, said through the screen. 'What will you have, young man?'

'My name is Kildare,' he began, 'I would like—'

'I know your name well enough,' she said bitterly. 'I wish to the kind God that I'd never heard it. You're the one who tries to frighten people to death, aren't you?'

'I've come to see Mr Winslow,' he said.

'I'll never let you come within a thousand miles of him!' she declared. She pushed the door almost shut. 'Not while I have my wits about me,' she added.

Kildare opened the screen and pushed the door wide against the resistance of the woman.

'I'll call in the neighbours. I'll scream!' she told him, the excitement shutting away her breath so that she hardly could whisper.

'I'm going to give him a chance to live,' said Kildare. 'Will you let me do that?'

She began to wring her hands. The dry skin sounded like paper.

'It was only anger that made you talk in that wild way to Geoffrey,' she said pleadingly. 'There wasn't any truth about—about what might happen before Monday?'

'I told him the truth,' said Kildare. 'I want to save him from it, if you'll let me.'

He had to catch her by the elbows to steady her, but she rallied herself quickly, her lips parted.

'I'll take you to him,' she said.

He went up the stairs behind her. In the upper hall she paused at a door and looked with a sort of woeful doubt toward Kildare. Then she knocked and opened the door a trifle.

'Geoffrey,' she said, 'may I bring him in?'

'What him?' asked Winslow.

'The man who said it—the man who said the thing to you, Geoffrey!'

'Get him out of my thought and out of my house,' commanded Winslow.

She glanced at Kildare again, making a gesture of surrender. Kildare walked through the door and closed it behind him.

A small coal fire burned in the grate across the room and Winslow was slouched down in an easy chair just before it. He started up out of the chair when he saw Kildare.

He was as if an outer garment of flesh had dropped away from him. He had been on the verge of an angry outburst of words; but now he controlled himself and began to gather his dignity coldly around him.

Kildare said: 'You're too weak, just now, to throw me out of your house. Will you let me try to explain why I'm here? A doctor takes an oath to heal where and when he can; and you're dying of a most violent form of pernicious anaemia, Mr Winslow. Will you let me help you?'

'A man's life isn't long enough,' said Winslow, 'for him to be changing his mind and changing his mind. I've spoken my thought about you and the rest of them, and I haven't changed.'

'Sit down,' invited Kildare. 'Because I intend to stay here a while and argue the point with you.'

When Kildare came out of the house into the downpour, he was joined instantly by Davison, wet as a drowned rat, his hat knocked out of shape and hanging down over his eyes.

'You ought to be back there with Joan,' said Kildare. 'What are you doing out here?'

'There was a queer look about you when you left the Lancey house,' said Davison, 'so I trailed you along to see what you were about to do. No matter what I expected you to do, I never expected to see you get into Winslow's cave. What have you been doing to the old

125

devil? Arguing?'

'In a way,' said Kildare.

'Well, admit that you lost your point.'

'I probably did,' said Kildare. 'What else is eating you, Jack?'

'Your father has just come in at the Lancey house,' said Davison. 'He wanted some drugs and odds and ends before he goes back on his rounds through Medwick. I thought you'd want to see him before he left.'

'Is he all in?' asked Kildare.

He looked straight before him and gripped his jaws hard together.

'He's not as bad as you think,' said Davison, 'but he needs some attention.'

'I'll attend to him,' said Kildare.

He found his father in the kitchen of the Lancey house pouring into a tin cup coffee which he had just brewed.

The nozzle of the pot chattered against the edge of the cup, in his trembling hands.

'Ah, Jimmy,' he said. 'Ah, my boy—here you are again! I just dropped in for a swallow of coffee...'

There was something about him infinitely apologetic, and shrinking, as if he wished to dodge even the eye of his son.

Kildare pretended not to look at him.

He merely said: 'How are things going?'

'Quite briskly,' said the father. 'Quite a few calls made and just a few more to finish off with before I go home.'

126

'Were you home yesterday?' asked Kildare.

'Why, yes, certainly,' said the father.

'And slept home last night?'

'As a matter of fact I had to telephone to your mother that I was held up. However, I had an excellent sleep as it was.'

'How long?' asked Kildare.

'Well, quite a few hours. Now I'll just swallow this and trot along about my business.'

'Wait a moment,' said Kildare.

'There's no use arguing with me, Jimmy,' he answered. 'If you and your men can't get at these people, I must do my best...'

'I'm not arguing,' said Kildare. 'Of course they need help and someone has to give it to them. There's an old Hippocrates and all that to remember, naturally. I was just thinking of something that might brace you up quite a bit for your rounds. Let me give you a couple of these in your coffee.'

'What are they, Jimmy?'

'That's a secret of my own. If you like the effect, I'll tell you about it.'

'You're not forming a habit of relying on drugs, Jimmy?'

'Not a chance, I take these when I've got to get through something. That's all.'

'In that case I might try them. One, I think. Just one, Jimmy.'

'Very well,' said Kildare, and pinching two of the pills together, he dropped them together into the coffee.

'Now sit down and wait till the stuff takes hold on you,' he directed. 'It gives you a rather drowsy sense, first. Just relax and let it take hold. You rouse out of it like a new man.'

'Not strychnine?' asked the father. 'Not strychnine combined with some hypnotic?'

'You've never heard of this sort of thing as a stimulant,' said Kildare. 'It's completely new.'

'Very well,' said the father, and drank the coffee down.

'Just sit there for five or ten minutes,' said Kildare.

'I'm a good patient, Jimmy. I'll follow orders.'

He relaxed in the chair. It was growing dusk. A moment later Midge Whalen came into the dim doorway.

'Doctor Carew wants you on the telephone,' he said. Kildare walked into the hall. 'I'm sorry that I let my tongue get away from me,' said Whalen. 'I'm going to stick this out to the last man.'

'I knew you weren't a rat,' said Kildare. 'Forget about it. Besides, there's a ghost of a chance that the ship won't sink, after all.'

'Really?'

'Yes. Tell the others. Tell Joan Davison, most of all.'

'What's the reason?'

'It's not a thing I can tell you, it's so far-fetched. Be a good fellow and wink at them and make a mystery of it, as if you were in the know.'

'I'll do that,' said Whalen, laughing.

On the telephone Carew said: 'Kildare, where have you been? I've gone out of my mind trying to reach you. I telephoned to the university. You were right. God forgive me, my boy hasn't appeared at his college since I talked with him!'

'I'm sorry for you, sir,' said Kildare.

'Oh, damn sorrow and me! Perhaps I *am* damned. Kildare, will you help me? Will you come back here and help me to get on the trail?'

'Isn't there a sign of them?'

There was a silence. Then the controlled voice said: 'Not a single sign.'

'You tried her place?'

'There was not a hint in her place of where they might have gone. Only a strong hint that they had left.'

'What sort of a hint?'

'Apparently everything in the place had been sold to second-hand dealers, or pawned. Kildare, you have a devilish faculty of seeing through the moves and motives of people. Will you come help me, my dear boy? Or must I call in the police?'

'Don't call in the police. The law can't stop them, you know.'

'I understand that. They're a law to themselves, now.'

'I'll be there tomorrow, if things go well

129

out here.'

'What things?'

'It's a long story. There's a ghost of a chance that I may be through here and then I'll come straight to you, sir.'

'God bless you, Kildare. But listen to me: *must* you stay there? You can't come straight to me this moment?'

'It has to do with the welfare of the whole town, sir.'

There was another long pause.

'You're right, of course ... Kildare!'

'Yes, sir.'

'Kildare, will they...'

'I don't think so,' lied Kildare in a strong voice. 'I think that they'll linger out all the moments that are left to them.'

Afterward, Kildare called the hospital back and spoke to Molly Cavendish. 'Mary Lamont has gone on vacation, hasn't she?'

'She's gone on something,' said Molly Cavendish. 'Vacation you may call it. She has a good deal to rest up from—and well you know it!'

'Has she gone up to Vermont?'

'I don't know. How should I know and why should I care?'

'Wire her right away and tell her that I want her back at the hospital tomorrow.'

'I'll do nothing of the kind,' said Molly Cavendish. 'The child has a right...'

'Never mind her rights. Send the wire.'

'Not even Dr Carew has a right to call a nurse in off vacation!'

'Dr Carew can do his own worrying. I'll do mine. Just send that wire, please!'

'I'll do it, then,' said the Cavendish, 'and a fine slap in the face I hope you'll get for it!'

Kildare returned to the kitchen and found that his father had fallen into a profound sleep, almost dropping out of his chair. He lifted the frail body in his arms and carried it from the room.

... The dusk turned to night and Stephen Kildare slept. His son telephoned to Dartford: 'He's resting. Mother. He'll be a better looking man tomorrow than he is today.'

'Jimmy, what are *you* doing in Medwick? What will Dr Gillespie have to say about you out there in Medwick?'

'I'll take care of myself. I know how to fall on my feet.'

'You'll watch your poor, silly, dear father, Jimmy?'

'I'll watch him, Mother.'

'There was that sweet thing, that Mary Lamont, here today.'

'Mary—in our house?'

'Yes. She was taking a message to you, dear. Did you see her?'

'I was busy, it seems, when she came,' said Kildare, heavily. 'But what did you talk to her about, Mother?'

'Talk to her? Oh, about nothing much—

131

except that Beatrice dropped in. I talked about Beatrice.'

'Oh, you talked about Beatrice?'

'What do you think? She found that old fishing rod of yours that's been lost so long! Bless her, what a girl she is, Jimmy!'

After that Kildare had the night to wait through. He kept a chair at the side of his father and dozed, from time to time, but now and again he slipped the card from Mary out of his pocket and glanced over what she had written.

It was the longest night of his life.

CHAPTER FIFTEEN

STAND UP, KILDARE!

There are two entrances to the town hall at Medwick. One is at the ground level and through it the townsfolk alone may pass. In more than a hundred years, it is said, no one except the men of Medwick have set foot upon that floor. None except the men of Medwick have sat on the speakers' platform at the end of the hall.

The second entrance gives upon a narrow stairway which leads up to a visitors' gallery where strangers as well as the women and children of the town may gather. On important occasions, even this gallery is cleared, and the minds of Medwick meditate their own affairs strictly by themselves.

In this gallery, today, sat Kildare with his five doctors like a small island surrounded by the females of Medwick. He and his men were so unpopular that a little open space was left around them on the ranged seats.

Since Kildare was in the front row of this balcony, he was plainly visible to all except those who remained standing directly under the gallery itself; and everyone, now and then, looked back and up at the strangers and many smiles and chuckles were exchanged until the presiding officer entered.

This was Winslow—Geoffrey Winslow, leading citizen and town banker—who appeared with a heavy suitcase in his hand and walked up the central aisle with a brisk step. His manner and bearing were so full of vigour that people stood up to stare at him.

And then the heads were sure to turn and leer at Kildare in the balcony; for the Monday prophecy was known to every person in the town.

Winslow climbed the steps to the speakers' platform, deposited and opened his suitcase, which seemed to be filled with papers, and then stood over against a small Franklin stove which warmed that end of the hall. Its grate was open and showed a mouth filled with yellow fire.

Winslow approached the stove and extended his hands toward the heat of it; at the same moment the whole audience rose, instinctively, and broke into a hearty applause of cheers and handclapping. This noise Winslow acknowledged by turning his stern head and nodding briefly at the crowd.

After this he lifted his hand, secured instant silence, and then stepped to the lectern which stood toward the edge of the platform.

'My friends,' he said, 'we will come to order. I am glad to be with you. I hope it will not be the last time in spite of what has been said about next Monday.'

A good, hearty booing followed this remark, though there was not a sign of a smile on the face of Winslow.

He rapped for order and said: 'Will someone move to dispense with the reading of the minutes of the last meeting?'

This was done. The men of Medwick sat back and waited for their leader. Still many an ominous or sneering glance was turned up toward Kildare, in that prominent first row of the balcony.

Winslow went on in a brisk, sharp way that was characteristic of him: 'Since the thought of death was forced upon me, it caused me to think over what I should do in my last days.'

More laughter interrupted him here, and he had to whack his gavel down to gain silence once more. The women near Kildare were

134

staring at him as if he were a strange animal.

'It occurred to me,' continued Winslow, 'that although I've spent my life in our town and tried to be a just man, still a great many people would be relieved when I died.'

There was a tumult of many voices that called out: 'That's not true! ... That's not a fact, Mr Winslow ... We can't listen to this sort of thing...'

'Nevertheless,' said Winslow, 'it *is* true. No man can enjoy being in debt, and too large a percentage of Medwick owes me money.'

This remark secured a very deep silence indeed.

'The fact is,' said Winslow, 'that as I meditated on the thought of death, I discovered that I did not mind dying so much as I minded having people happy because of that death; and this put me to thinking out my affairs in quite a different way.

'I'd never looked at the business of the world so clearly as when I seemed about to leave it. For the first time, it was clear to me that enough money to house and clothe and feed a man should also be enough to content him; it gives him a free mind, and that freedom is what we ought to pursue and envy and aspire toward.

'I remembered, then, that I have enough invested capital left to take care of me and my family even without the debts which are owed to me in the town. So I decided that when I came here today, I would tell you people of Medwick that you helped me to build up my little fortune, and that it is only right that part of it should go back to you.

'I have here in this suitcase the only records of money owing to me from the people of Medwick; and I now blot out those records.'

With this, he picked up a double handful of the papers in the suitcase and thrust them into the mouth of the Franklin stove.

The great heat and the opened draft caused the dry paper to go up in roaring flame at once, so that Winslow was able to dip out one mass after another of the bills until his suitcase was emptied except for a small sheaf of papers which he reserved in his hand.

The second or the third portion of the bills had gone up in flames before the bewildered people of Medwick understood exactly what was happening. A woman in the balcony cupped her hands at her mouth and yelled through this trumpet: 'Mark! Mark! Oh, Mark Williams! There's our barn and cow come back to us! Oh, Mark Williams! Oh, Mark!'

There was no laughter to greet this outburst. Single voices and then a whole chorus broke out. Men stood up on the floor of the hall and waved frantically to their wives in the balcony; and the wives nodded and waved back in an ecstasy. Many of them burst into loud weeping.

Long after Winslow had finished this

sacrifice, the tumult still continued. Several men ran out of the meeting house to carry the great tidings to their families. More would have gone, except that the sergeant-at-arms barred the way and stood guard over it.

'What is it, Jimmy?' asked Davison, close to his friend. 'Has the old boy gone out of his head?'

'I don't know,' said Kildare. 'I've never seen anything like it.'

'Sounds like he had religion.'

'He's had religion all his life,' said Kildare. 'I can't make this out.'

The sight of Winslow standing erect at the lectern with the small sheaf of papers remaining in his hand gradually brought the audience back to attention. When, by degrees, the uproar had died down, Winslow was saying:

'I excepted a few of the debts from the crowd. Because I think that there are some of you who can well afford to pay a part of your debts, at least.

'The fact is that I have a purpose of raising a new building in Medwick. It is something which we have needed bitterly for a long time, and I propose that we shall make a united effort to that end.

'To begin with, I want to know whether either Mr Reed or Mr Minter, of the building firm of Reed and Minter, may be here.'

'Here, sir'—'Here, Mr Winslow,' said two

men, standing up.

'If I cross out half of your debt, my friends,' said Winslow, 'and let you turn in the rest in the shape of bricks and cement, do you think it will be fair?'

'More than fair, sir,' said Minter. 'We haven't a right—'

'Nobody has a right but Medwick; nobody has a real claim on any one of his fellow townsmen,' said Winslow. 'What we are, the town has made us. And now that Medwick is weakening, we are going to rally to her support, are we not?'

There was another great shouting at this; but people waited in excitement to learn the full purpose of Winslow, and the shouting died down almost at once.

'I want other help,' said Winslow. 'Mr Brace, are you here? Oliver Brace?'

A fat man arose, helping himself up on the back of the chair in front of him.

'Kind of winded, Mr Winslow, but still mostly here,' said Brace.

'We want a slate roof on this building,' said Winslow. 'Your debt is cancelled if you'll put it on for me.'

'Why, God bless you,' said Brace, 'I'm the happiest man in Medwick, even if I have to cover a building from here to the river!'

'What's the building to be, Mr Winslow? What's the building to be?' voices began to call.

Winslow crumpled the rest of the bills in his

138

hand and tossed them into the open mouth of the stove, now filled with a charred mass of friable carbon.

'There's no use making bargains,' he said, 'because I know that we're standing together in this work, shoulder to shoulder, and shame will make the men work, whether they love Medwick or not. Now, I want to tell you what the new building is to be, the thing which we most seriously need. It's to be a hospital, my friends, to take care—'

A shout broke in upon him. Instant silence followed.

'We are going to take care of our young and old,' said Winslow. 'We've been careless and slack too long. We've been too proud of our town and its merits. But now we're going to take care of Medwick and of all the people in it.

'We're not going to use our own prejudiced opinions but we're going to use opinions of professionally educated men, who know what they're talking about. When they tell us that Medwick is up to standard, we'll relax a little.

'Until that time we're going to keep working, in the knowledge that hard times cannot last forever, and that if we make Medwick fit for better things, better things will come to her.'

He paused and took a visible long breath. There was at each pause the excited shout and then silence.

'For doctors,' said Winslow, 'We want the best that we can find, that is to say, the best we can find at a price we can afford to pay. Five dollars a head is enough to insure a minimum of good medical service. I'm asking someone to propose that the town be taxed ten cents a head a week. Do I hear such a motion?'

It was made and passed in a moment, a very loud moment of roaring responses.

'Now I must tell you,' said Winslow, 'what gave me my second chance at life, what brought me here to cancel the debts that have been burdening you, and what makes me ask you to work with me shoulder to shoulder in giving to our town a proper medical service.

'My friends, I sat in my house slowly dying, yesterday, and I had given up all hope of life when a man came to me whom I had blocked, cheated, and made small of; and yet his only crime against all of us is youth.

'He risked his own career to help us. He insisted on doing us good when we refused him. And in spite of my insults and my contempt he forced me to listen to him yesterday evening; he forced his treatment on me; he gave me back life as if by a miracle ... Stand up, Doctor Kildare!'

At this sudden appeal, Kildare sat stunned; but Davison on one side and Whalen on the other boosted him violently to his feet.

This stroke of the spotlight full upon him made Kildare hang his head like a backward

140

child being reproved by a school teacher; but this awkwardness was something which the men and women of Medwick were able to understand perfectly. Modesty is the most charming of all virtues to Americans.

The voice of Winslow, higher and more dominant than ever, went on: 'This man brought to us his associates, chosen young doctors full of energy, too honest to flatter us, insisting on telling us the truth.

'We called it witchcraft, but it was only honest science which is more interested in preventing than in curing disease. We laughed at these brave and generous young men; we have kept on laughing at them; but since my life has been given back to me, I'm asking you to let them help you as they've helped me.

'*They* are the staff for our hospital. My friends, do you accept them?'

Nothing could have bewildered the people of Medwick more than this sudden transition of villain into hero.

But they were too accustomed to the third acts of melodramas to be entirely surprised by it; and in fact Winslow had so staged the speech that it was very like a stage effect that he offered now to his townsmen.

They were already on their feet both in the gallery and on the floor of the meeting house. A murmur that began to rise among them now broke out in heartier applause than ever greeted the fall of a third act curtain when the

141

heroine is saved, the villain foiled, and the hero triumphant.

Davison, as the uproar grew, began to laugh hysterically. When at last they reached the street, a tide of smiling faces and happy tumult accompanied them even to the door of the Lancey house.

The noise brought Joan Davison's frightened face to an upstairs window; and only by degrees the full, happy comprehension dawned on her.

She hurried as fast as she could downstairs where the corps of young doctors was coming into the hall, slapping each other on the shoulders, and laughing like children.

Only Kildare was as grave as a face of stone among them. The girl pushed by her husband without a glance and went straight toward the interne.

CHAPTER SIXTEEN

LOST LADY

It was early afternoon of the day, when Kildare got back to the hospital and reported at his office.

'What are you doing in street clothes?' demanded Gillespie. 'Climb into your working togs and get up to Operating Room Number 7.

There's a beautiful double mastoid about to go on there, and I want you to see it...

'But you had some luck out there in Medwick, didn't you?'

'Luck?' said Kildare, a little bewildered.

'Why, certainly,' growled Gillespie. 'You find your villain out there with pernicious anaemia, and a big injection of liver extract turns him into a different man over night. Is that luck, or not?'

'How do you keep in touch with everything as closely as that?' asked Kildare.

'I'll tell you how,' said Gillespie. 'It's a rare gift, and I'll tell you about it. As a matter of fact, it's something that only God can give you. Do you know what it is?'

'No, sir,' said Kildare.

'I'll tell you, then. God gave me two eyes, two ears, and a damned long nose—and I use God's gifts. That's all there is to it ... Now get up to that operating room.'

'There's one more thing that I ought to do, sir.'

'Stand on your head, or what?'

'Dr Carew wishes me to—'

'If Carew wants you, that's enough for me. Run along about his business and then get back here as fast as the Lord will let you. We've lost days, Jimmy. We've lost whole days, and time is the only thing that can't be bought and paid for!'

He went on into the other office in time to see

143

Mary Lamont coming through the opposite door, wearing street clothes. The sight of him stopped her. Something rose in the heart of Kildare and almost reached his lips in a rush of words. He choked it back.

'Molly Cavendish said that you needed me for some emergency work?' she asked, distant and strangely judicial.

'Did you have to come a long way?' he wanted to know.

'It's all right, if there's really an emergency,' she said.

'I knew they'd do something to us,' said Kildare watching her.

'Do something? Who?'

'Young Carew and the girl. Whoever is wrong, you and I know that they're right. I suppose there's only one way of being right. Is that it, Mary?'

She was silent, either because she did not wish to hurt him or because her mind was not entirely sure.

Kildare interpreted himself. 'They can't live without each other. But I can live without you and you without me. That means we're wrong?'

She was silent still.

'It's queer,' said Kildare. 'I can see through other people, sometimes, but I never can see through you. I can't tell what's in your mind, now. I haven't the foggiest idea.'

'I don't think talking does much good,' she

said. 'We know each other's ideas too well.'

'I can see something now,' said Kildare. 'You're trying to be insouciant, but all the while you're a bit frightened. Isn't that true?'

'Yes,' she said.

'Well, I'll say nothing more to frighten you. I want you to help me find Marguerite and young Carew. How well did you get to know her when you called?'

'I couldn't get to know her very well. She doesn't live in my world, Jimmy.'

'She won't die in our world, either,' said Kildare. 'No matter what the newspapers may think, I want to go to her room now. Will you go along?'

'Jimmy—'

'Yes?'

'I'm afraid of it.'

'Why?'

'I suppose you'll run them down. There's a sort of bloodhound in you that never misses a trail. But you won't find them living, Jimmy. I know you won't, and I'm afraid of it! Please don't make me!'

'I can't make you do anything,' said Kildare. 'We'll just drop all this.'

'No, I'll come.'

'You look sick.'

'I *am* sick.'

'Then you stay out of this, Mary.'

'No. Nothing could keep me out of it, now.

I'll be all right. I just had to *say* it, I suppose.'

'Will I ever understand you?' asked Kildare.

'I don't think so,' said Mary.

The janitor of the tenement house knew Kildare. That was why they got the key so readily to the room of Marguerite Paston. The janitor said: 'Why you wanta get into her room, Doc?'

'You don't want to know that,' said Kildare.

'All right,' said the janitor, 'I didn't even ask.'

He went up the stairs before them and opened a door.

'Do I hang around and keep my eyes open?' asked the janitor.

'No, you go away and keep your eyes shut.'

'Okay,' said the janitor. 'Drop in and see Dick Loring on the third floor, some time, will you? He's kind of red and swole up. Maybe from the gin, or something.'

'He makes his own, doesn't he?'

'Yeah; what do you think?'

'I'll drop in on him, some day,' said Kildare.

'Thanks,' said the janitor. 'It don't do no good to a house to have the mugs croak in it. It gives people ideas, I dunno why.'

Then they were alone in the room. It had a steam radiator, a narrow chest-of-drawers, an iron bed, two chairs, an oblong of matting beside the bed.

Kildare stood in the middle of the floor and looked around him. Down in the street a

146

newsboy was sing-songing an extra, his voice like the crow of a rooster.

'Look in the closet,' said Kildare, and went over to the bureau.

'There's an old hat and an umbrella in here. That's all,' said Mary Lamont.

'There's a lot of lingerie in the bureau, still,' said Kildare. 'Handkerchiefs, too, and all that sort of thing ... Are there any shoes in the closet?'

'Yes. I didn't see them before.'

'She didn't try to move out everything.'

'No, only what she'd need before—'

'Don't get soft, now. Remember you're a trained nurse.'

'I won't get soft,' said Mary Lamont, taking a quick breath.

Kildare pulled a small snapshot from the back of a drawer, where it had slipped into a crack. It was a good likeness of the heads of young Carew and the girl, close together.

He stood back with the picture in his hand; into his absent mind the crowing voice of the newsboy kept entering.

'I've got to get something out of this,' said Kildare.

'How can you?' asked Mary Lamont.

'I don't know. We've got almost no cards, here, so I've got to play this one big.'

'You can't buy a dollar's worth with a nickel, can you, Jimmy?'

'Sometimes,' said Kildare.

147

He sat down and stared at the picture.

'I'm the one who did it to them.'

'Jimmy! No, no!' she cried.

'I did it to them,' said Kildare. 'I could have made Carew understand before they went back to him. But I took it for granted. If I ever take anything for granted again...'

'Jimmy, it isn't right for you to suffer like this. Nobody could say that it's your fault.'

'Everything is your fault, if you could have prevented it.'

'That sort of thinking will drive you crazy.'

'That's the way I'm going to keep on thinking, though.

'You stay here and keep on looking,' he commanded, going to the door.

'Jimmy?'

'Well?'

'I don't want to be alone in this room. I can't breathe in it.'

'You stay here and make yourself like it. I'll leave the door open. I've never seen you act up like this before.'

'I won't act up any more,' she agreed.

He went down to the street and said to the newsboy who was still crowing: 'Seen Red?'

'Sure, Doc,' said the newsboy. 'I seen him go into Slater's for a hot-dog. Red eats about twenty hot-dogs a day.'

The scrawny figure of Red was perched on a stool at the lunch counter of Slater's munching a hot-dog that dripped yellow mustard.

'You like that much mustard?' asked Kildare.

'Hi, doc! Sit down and have one on me, will you?' demanded Red, leaping up.

'No, I won't have anything. Take it easy. Like that much mustard?'

'No,' said Red, 'but it's free.'

'How was Christmas?'

'Lousy,' said Red.

'Why?'

'I've grown up out of tin. Tin junk don't make no Christmas for me, no more. And the kind of Santa Clause we got in our place don't carry nothing else. Not on twenty a week he don't.'

'Look at this picture,' said Kildare.

'Yeah?'

'Ever see them around here?'

'Nope ... She's got a kind of a look, ain't she? Moving picture star or something?'

'No, Red, take another think. What's the worst thing that you see on the streets?'

'A run-over cat. They kind of squash out.'

'What's the next worst?'

'I dunno, doc. The spoony loonies, maybe?'

'The couples that go strolling around?'

'Yeah, or sitting. They got a kind of a gone look like they been hit on the head. Walking or sitting, they dunno where they are.'

'Look at these people again. Remember them now, walking together?'

'Doggone me if I don't, now. Walking close

149

together, dead slow. They were different.'

'How different?'

'They didn't lean on each other. They acted like they had two pair of feet. They didn't keep grinning at each other, either. They looked straight ahead, as if they were going somewhere and there wasn't no hurry. Are they a pair of dopes, too, like the rest of them?'

'The worst dopes you ever saw,' said Kildare.

'You wouldn't think it,' said Red.

'I'm hunting for them, Red. Help me?'

'Whatta you think?'

'All right. Scram. Here's a dollar for expenses.'

'I don't have no expenses, when I'm working for you.'

'Get some of the other boys to help out. It may be a long trail, Red.'

'I'll get my gang,' said Red.

'And don't stop because your feet get tired.'

'My feet don't get that way.'

'Take this fifty cents, anyway. When you and the boys get thirsty, I mean.'

'It don't look like real money to me,' said Red.

'All right, Red. When you come back, you'll find me at Mike's.'

'They don't leave me come in there no more,' said Red.

'They'll let you come in if you ask for me.'

'Sure they will,' said Red. 'So long, doc.'

Kildare went back to the room of Marguerite Paston. He found Mary Lamont highly excited and a little frightened still.

'A girl went into the door across the hall,' she said. 'She was wearing a coat like Marguerite's.'

'Did you speak to her?'

'Oh, no!'

'Listen to me, Mary. People in places like this don't bite if you speak to them.'

'I don't mind them—when they're in the hospital,' said Mary.

'You'll get over minding them, outside the hospital, too,' said Kildare, 'or else you'll never amount to a damn.'

He turned back as he reached the door.

'You've got tears in your eyes,' he said. 'Did I hurt your feelings?'

'No,' she said.

'Why the tears, then?'

'I'm catching a bit of a cold, I think.'

He turned slowly and went on across the hall. When he knocked at the door a voice sang out: 'Hey—come in!'

He opened the door. The girl lay on the bed with her knees hunched up. Her face was obscured by the comic section she was reading.

'Jeez, you're getting polite, Barney,' she said. 'Knocking at the door and everything. Take the weight off your feet.'

Kildare sat down. He lighted a cigarette.

'Gimme one, too,' said the voice from

behind the paper. 'Bring any beer?'

'No,' said Kildare.

She lowered the paper, slowly. She eyed Kildare thoughtfully. She was very thin and very pretty. Careless use of the lipstick made her mouth seem clumsy and wet.

'What's the gag?' she asked.

Kildare pointed to the red-checked coat that lay across a chair.

'Did she give it to you or did you borrow it?' he asked.

The girl said nothing. She kept on surveying him, without altering her position.

Kildare offered her a cigarette. She took it. He gave it a light and tossed the match away. He sat down again.

'Loan or gift?' asked Kildare.

'What are you talking about, bozo?' she asked.

'The girl across the hall,' said Kildare.

'I dunno any girl across the hall,' she said.

'She knew you.'

'Yeah. A lot of people know me, not including you.'

'She used to talk about you.'

'Did she?'

'Yes.'

'That was a waste of time.'

'She didn't think so.'

'This one across the hall, what did she have to say about me?'

'She said that you weren't too hard

152

to break.'

'How break?'

'Break down.'

'Maybe you think so.'

'When I saw you in her coat, I thought you might talk to me about her, a little.'

'I dunno who you mean,' said the girl. 'Where are you going?'

'Across town a ways.'

'Why don't you go there, then?'

'Mary!' called Kildare.

Mary Lamont came to the open door.

'Hey, what is this, anyway?' asked the girl.

'Close the door,' said Kildare. Mary came in and shut it behind her.

'How do you do?' said Mary.

'I don't do so bad,' said the girl. 'What are you birds after, anyway?'

'What's your name?' asked Kildare.

'Sadie.'

'Sadie never saw Marguerite,' said Kildare. 'She never borrowed or took the coat. She doesn't know anything.'

'Are you a female dick, Mary?' asked Sadie.

'No. I'm a nurse in the hospital. This is Dr Kildare, Sadie.'

'So what?'

'I thought you might have heard of him,' said Mary. She smiled. Sadie did not smile back.

'As long as you're here, you might as well sit down,' said Sadie.

153

'No. I don't want to bother you ... We're not here to make any trouble.'

'Not much. You're here just for fun, aren't you?' asked Sadie.

'No, we came here to ask you about Marguerite's trip,' said Kildare.

'I don't know nothing about any trip,' declared Sadie.

'I wondered how long you thought it would last,' said Kildare. 'Or do you think that she'll ever come back?'

'From where?' asked Sadie.

'Does she intend to die?' asked Kildare, gently.

'How would I know that about whom?' cried Sadie. She jumped up and hooked a thumb at the door. 'Barge out of here, you mugs, will you? How would I know about anybody dying?'

'Shall I tell you?' asked Kildare.

'Yeah? What could you tell me?'

'Will you go back to Marguerite's room for a moment?' asked Kildare.

Mary Lamont went out, quietly.

'It don't matter whether we're alone or not,' said Sadie. 'I don't want you to hold my hand, Flat-face. But go on and tell me what I would know about anybody going and dying?'

'Because you've thought of it for yourself, Sadie, haven't you?' he asked.

The answer remained on her parted lips,

unspoken.

He went on: 'So even though Marguerite didn't say anything to you, you knew what she had in mind, didn't you?'

Sadie took breath.

'Did she go and do it, poor kid?' she whispered.

'I don't know,' said Kildare. 'I'm trying to find her, Sadie. Will you help me with anything you know?'

'Who *are* you?' demanded Sadie.

'I'm nobody,' said Kildare. 'I'm only an interne in the hospital.'

'Wait a minute,' said Sadie. 'Are you, maybe, the doc?'

'Some of the people call me that,' said Kildare.

'Sure, you're the doc,' said Sadie. She went over to Kildare and faced him closely. 'Why be dumb?' she asked. 'Why not tell me from the start? Sure you're the doc. You talk the way they say you do. You don't want anything except to help her, do you?'

'That's all,' said Kildare.

'Gimme another cigarette,' said Sadie. 'I wish I had a drink, too. I need one, when I think about that poor gal. My God, doc, she's the only one that's like herself.'

'I think she is,' said Kildare.

'All I know is this,' said Sadie, 'I met up with her a coupla three times in the hall and she smiled at me. She's friendly, that's what she is.

155

'Then we started talking a coupla times. She found out that I didn't have any extra heavy coats, so she slipped me this for Christmas.

'It's a funny thing. Bar none, it's the first thing that any *woman* ever gave me.

'And then the other day she gave me this and asked me to mail it not later than today—this is Thursday, isn't it? To be sure and mail it not before today, and not any later.'

She opened her purse. She took out a handkerchief, unfolded it, and took out an envelope.

'Wanta look?' she asked.

'No,' said Kildare.

'She wouldn't mind *you* seeing it,' said Sadie.

'Not before Thursday, not after Thursday,' murmured Kildare. 'Then I suppose that this is the day, Sadie?'

'The day for what?' she asked. Then, as realisation came to her, she drew breath through her teeth, hunching up her shoulders and wincing.

'I didn't think of that,' she said.

'You've helped me a lot,' said Kildare, holding out his hand. 'You've given me a time limit.'

He went back to Mary Lamont and said: 'It will happen today. Before night comes, I suppose. If they arranged a day in their own minds, they wouldn't wait till the darkness, do you think?'

'No,' said Mary, shuddering. 'They

156

wouldn't wait for a winter night.'

'I don't need you, now,' said Kildare. 'I have to do the rest of this alone.'

They went down to the street together.

'Half of the afternoon is gone already,' said Mary. '*What* can you do, Jimmy?'

'Spend some time waiting,' said Kildare. 'Will you be in the hospital?'

'Yes. Jimmy, if I ever thought that you weren't—weren't—I don't know how to say it, but I was wrong!'

CHAPTER SEVENTEEN

THE HANDS OF KILDARE

The rain cleared off a little later, so that the ending of this December day promised to be as bright as summer.

There was less than an hour before sundown when Mike kicked open the door of the family room where Kildare sat alone with his thoughts and said: 'Here's the worthless young rat, doc.'

Red came in with a swollen and rapidly purpling eye.

'How did it happen, Red?' asked Kildare.

'Over there on the East Side, I tell you what they got,' said Red. 'They got some good straight lefts! Before I could get at that mug, he

157

struck me in the eye with that left so often that I thought I was bumping my head against a wall.

'But finally I got inside and softened him up till he would talk. It was *him* that showed me the rest of the way to the water.'

'To the water?' repeated Kildare sharply.

'Yeah. To the East River. That was the last time that anybody noticed them. Over where those barges are all tied up in rows, you know?'

Kildare got there as fast as a taxicab would take him.

'One of the kids seen them walking right along here,' said Red, pointing down a street. 'Then nobody seen them no more. They didn't take a dive in the river, did they, Doc?'

'Wait here,' said Kildare, and went toward the barges.

Rusty-sided, big, shapeless, they crowded together like tethered animals. Each had its small caboose and from some of these wisps of smoke went up, and there was a random odour of cookery to blend with the smell of the sea.

People as battered as the barges appeared from the doors of the cabooses when Kildare asked questions. But no one had seen two youngsters such as Marguerite Paston and the boy.

He went on to the outer row of the barges, and to the one farthest west in the line. He had to move carefully; for there was plenty to stumble over, and the westering sun flamed straight in his eye, turning crimson above the

158

horizon.

He saw, beyond the caboose, two figures against the sky. The wind fanned to one side the skirt of the girl; then the feet of Kildare stumbled and came down hard on the deck.

When he looked up again, the pair were standing on the extreme bulwark of the barge, balancing uneasily with the sway of the waves. They clung close together, looking anxiously behind them toward Kildare.

He knew that they were one step from the end of their journey. He dared not move nearer; he hardly dared to speak; he could only take off his hat so that they might recognise him.

It seemed to him that each instant, as they stood wavering there, was the last; and with every motion of the barge on the tide they appeared to be throwing themselves into the current.

The girl stretched out a hand toward him. He could not tell whether it was in greeting or in a last farewell...

*   *   *

An east wind had brought the winter back on Manhattan when Kildare reached the office of Dr Carew that night.

Old Carew, standing up slowly behind his desk, rested his weight on his hands and stared speechlessly for a moment; Kildare stood with his head bowed, looking at the floor.

'It was no good, Kildare?' stammered the old doctor.

'I wonder,' said Kildare, 'even if I'd succeeded—would there have been any use?'

'Use? Isn't there use in life, man?' demanded Carew.

'Not if it means being jibed at and held in contempt and despised openly,' said Kildare. 'A life like that isn't worth anything.'

'It wouldn't be such a life, Jimmy,' said Carew. 'I've learned where I was wrong.'

'Can a man learn that, all in a moment?' said Kildare. 'Can you learn to understand a boy like your son, and his pride, and all that makes him different from you and me? Have you ever treated him as a man, instead of a child?'

'I can learn,' said Carew. 'I could begin now, Kildare, if God would give me some hope of seeing him again.'

'But you'd need patience with him,' said Kildare. 'Cold-blooded horses don't matter, but if you flog your thoroughbred, he'll jump over a cliff.'

'I know it now, Jimmy.'

'He can't be left to schools and teachers entirely. He has to be understood,' said Kildare. 'He can't be treated as something less than a human being.'

'I've been wrong,' said Carew. 'God knows how terribly I've been wrong.'

'Have you ever,' said Kildare, 'had one

close, human conversation with him? Have you ever been tired and unhappy in front of him—as my father has been, in front of me?'

'No,' murmured Carew. 'I've been no use to him; and he's been no use to me . . . But are you tormenting me for nothing, Jimmy? Is there any shadow or ghost of hope that I ever can see him again?'

Kildare stepped back to the door of the ante-room and opened it.

'I sent your secretary away, sir,' he said. 'They're waiting for you and a new chance in here, Dr Carew.'

Carew ran like a boy from behind the desk, across the office to the ante-room door. He had a frightened, hunted look.

And Kildare saw young Carew, against the wall of the ante-room, putting the girl behind him, as if to stand between her and a hostile force.

Carew must have understood that gesture, also, for he gave a strange cry and hurried forward with his arms outstretched.

Kildare shut the door soundlessly behind him.

When Kildare reached the office of Gillespie again, he was in hospital whites. He found the line stalled in the big waiting-room.

'Go in soft and easy, doc,' said Conover. 'Dr Gillespie is sitting and thinking. You know what that means.'

In fact Gillespie did not look up until

Kildare was half across the room.

'Poor Walter!' said Gillespie. 'Poor Walter Carew! ... God forgive you, Jimmy. You've handed Carew something to think about the rest of his days, and shame himself with, too. But he'll have to thank you for it...

'It's a queer thing, Jimmy, that your hands don't look any bigger than they did yesterday, and yet they've had three lives in them!...

'Now go get those Livingston reports—on the run, Kildare! We've got to make up time; we've got to make up time!'

As Kildare left for the inner office, he heard Gillespie muttering: 'God pity all fathers; God pity all sons!'

In the inner office he found Mary Lamont, also back in hospital whites.

'But what about your vacation, Mary?' he asked her.

'Do I help you here, Jimmy?' she asked.

'God knows you do,' he said.

'Then don't talk about vacations. I know what you've done—'

She choked.

'But do we know any more about one another than we did before?' he asked.

'No. I suppose not,' she said.

'Will we keep on wounding one another and misunderstanding?'

'Probably.'

'To the end of time?'

'To the very end,' said the girl.

162

'And you'll wish I were different and that everything were different?'

'Perhaps I shall.'

'Gillespie was saying something, just now,' murmured Kildare.

'I don't care about Gillespie. What are *you* thinking?'

'God pity all men; God pity all women,' said Kildare.

'Is that what Gillespie was saying?'

'I don't know. Perhaps. I don't feel that I know much of anything.'

He stood looking at her.

'Kildare! The Livingston reports, damn it!' roared Gillespie from the next room.

'Here they are,' said the girl, quickly.

'Thanks,' said Kildare. He took the reports, the clumsy, sprawling pack of cards, into his arms, and the girl with them.

Max Brand™ is the best-known pen name of Frederick Faust, creator of Dr Kildare,™ Destry, and many other fictional characters popular with readers and viewers worldwide. Faust wrote for a variety of audiences in many genres. His enormous output, totaling approximately thirty million words or the equivalent of 530 ordinary books, covered nearly every field: crime, fantasy, historical romance, espionage, Westerns, science fiction, adventure, animal stories, love, war, and fashionable society, big business and big medicine. Eighty motion pictures have been based on his work along with many radio and television programs. For good measure he also published four volumes of poetry. Perhaps no other author has reached more people in more different ways.

Born in Seattle in 1892, orphaned early, Faust grew up in the rural San Joaquin Valley of California. At Berkeley he became a student rebel and one-man literary movement, contributing prodigiously to all campus publications. Denied a degree because of unconventional conduct, he embarked on a series of adventures culminating in New York City where, after a period of near starvation, he received simultaneous recognition as a serious poet and successful popular-prose writer. Later, he traveled widely, making his home in New York, then in Florence, and finally in Los Angeles.

Once the United States entered the Second World War, Faust abandoned his lucrative writing career and his work as a screenwriter to serve as a war correspondent with the infantry in Italy, despite his fifty-one years and a bad heart. He was killed during a night attack on a hilltop village held by the German army. New books based on magazine serials or unpublished manuscripts continue to appear. Alive and dead he has averaged a new one every four months for seventy-five years. In the U.S. alone nine publishers issue his work, plus many more in foreign countries. Yet, only recently have the full dimensions of this extraordinarily versatile and prolific writer come to be recognized and his stature as a protean literary figure in the 20th Century acknowledged. His popularity continues to grow throughout the world.

We hope you have enjoyed this Large Print book. Other Chivers Press or G.K. Hall Large Print books are available at your library or directly from the publishers. For more information about current and forthcoming titles, please call or write, without obligation, to:

Chivers Press Limited
Windsor Bridge Road
Bath BA2 3AX
England
Tel. (01225) 335336

OR

G.K. Hall
P.O. Box 159
Thorndike, Maine 04986
USA
Tel. (800) 223–2336

All our Large Print titles are designed for easy reading, and all our books are made to last.